W9-AYS-799

A
Harlequin
Romance

RETURN TO DRAGONSHILL

by

ESSIE SUMMERS

HARLEQUIN BOOKS

Toronto • Canada   New York • New York

RETURN TO DRAGONSHILL

First published in 1971 by Mills & Boon Limited,
17 - 19 Foley Street, London, England

Harlequin Canadian edition published June, 1971
Harlequin U.S. edition published September, 1971

Standard Book Number: 373-51502-2.

To Bunty and Johnny Aldous
and Kitty Carter
of Ipswich, Suffolk, who
showed us some of the most
beautiful places in England
during a perfect English June

The author thanks the *Australian Woman's Mirror* for permission to quote verses from 'Who shall Sing' by C. McEwan.

CHAPTER ONE

HENRIETTA couldn't believe it when the phone rang again. She put down her eye-shadow for the fourth time and went into her living-room. This woman who kept ringing the wrong number must, now, ring the faults section of the exchange and complain. There were limits to one's patience.

She said her number again, crisply and extremely clearly.

And a voice, not a woman's, and one that turned her bones to water, said, 'Henrietta?'

It wasn't fair. It just wasn't fair. To recognize a voice so instantly after five years and still to know that traitor leap of the heart.

But he wasn't going to know that. Oh, no.

She said with a note of query, 'Yes?'

The voice laughed, continued, '*My* darling Henrietta?'

She allowed herself to sound puzzled, even amused. 'I wouldn't know. Who can be speaking?'

His voice was audacious, confident. It made Henrietta's blood boil. 'I'm sure you know. Who *could* it be but Johnny?'

She was rather proud of the way she reacted. No more, ever, was it going to be a case of 'Whistle and I'll come to ye, my lad.'

The bewilderment in her voice sounded completely genuine.

'I'm afraid that doesn't make it any clearer ... saying Johnny, I mean. I know at least three Johnnys in Wellington, but I can't think which of them would have the nerve to say I was *his* darling Henrietta!'

She hoped she'd made her point, but the voice still sounded assured. 'Henrietta, you goose, not from Wellington. From ... shall I say Dragonshill, even if I

7

have just flown in from the States? The Johnny that belongs in your life. Always has. Well, from schooldays on.'

Henrietta said, as if a great light had just dawned, 'Oh, good gracious ... you mean it's Johnny Carruthers! Oh, hullo, Johnny. Look, forgive me if I didn't catch on for the moment. I'm getting ready for a Trade Mission reception later tonight, and I have a lot on my mind. And someone called Johnny happens to be escorting me. Are you going to be in Wellington for a day or two, because I'd like to see you, but I'm afraid tonight is out of the——'

'Yes, I'll be here a day or two, but I'm coming right round—now, my girl.'

'I don't want to be delayed, Johnny. Can't you make it tomorrow. I——'

'I'm in Lambton Quay. I've only got to hop on the Cable Car. I know exactly where your flat is. I know Kelburn well. Don't fuss, I'll talk to you through the door while you're getting ready.'

Henrietta closed her eyes. She wanted time. Time to steel herself against the impact of Johnny's personality. Time to make sure her mask of sophistication was firmly in place.

She said crisply, 'I suppose I can't stop you if you're in one of your juggernaut moods, but you must understand I can't be delayed too long. I'm with what was called the External Affairs Department when you were in New Zealand last. There's a reception at the Royal Oak, and my job is to look after certain ones among the wives of the Trade Mission delegates. I'm not going in a private capacity, and unpunctuality is a cardinal sin in this job.'

He laughed. 'Your warmth of welcome overwhelms me! Good job I have a tough hide. I'll be with you in a quarter of an hour. *Au revoir,* my *darling* Henrietta.'

Henrietta replaced the receiver and sank down on the lambskin telephone stool.

Johnny! In a quarter of an hour. Her eyes went to

8

the clock. There would be more time alone with him than she desired ... or could bear. Time possibly for him to disarm her, to waken within her again all he had once meant to her.

A spark came into her eye. She picked up the phone again, dialled a number. 'John? Henrietta here. I wondered if you'd like to come rather earlier and have a glass of sherry first, here. Might fortify us for the evening ahead.'

'Rather. I'd have suggested it to you yesterday, but I had an idea you were going to start packing today.'

She said swiftly, 'I had intended to but couldn't be bothered. Oh, John, there'll be an old friend here. It's rather a nuisance. He's just flown in from the States. I—well, I can't explain now. But I'd rather he didn't know I'm giving up this job and going back to Dragonshill as their governess. So keep it to yourself, will you?' She paused, added: 'And I'd just as soon you didn't mention that it's not a long affair tonight. I don't want this chap on my doorstep when I come home.'

John said, 'I will, girl. By the way, I'll be bringing Jock with me. He came to my flat for a meal—his wife and children are out to tea—and his car has broken down, so he can come in the official car with us. Okay?'

Henrietta's voice warmed. 'That will be delightful. Good. Be seeing you, then.'

When she'd hung up she burst out laughing. John Durant and John McIntosh! If that didn't convince Johnny Carruthers there were more Johns than one she'd not seen for five years, what would?

Perhaps it was just as well someone had interrupted her packing this afternoon. There was just this one carton of books, half-packed. She bent, picked them out of the box, thrust them back on the shelves and carried the carton out to her fire-escape.

She quickly and expertly finished shadowing her eyelids, looked at herself in the mirror most critically, but was satisfied with what she saw ... very little here of the tomboyish Henrietta of earlier years ... that one had been ruffled, untidy, eager and ... very naïve.

This one looked smooth, cool, experienced. And ... well, quite attractive. Henrietta, confident in her outward appearance, schooled even that traitor heart of hers to stop racing.

She heard steps coming up her stairs, a tap at the door, and a quick turning of the handle. Johnny's voice said, 'Here I am,' as if she'd been standing waiting impatiently for his arrival!

Henrietta came through into her living-room in leisurely fashion, and despite the fact that the twilight had almost deepened into night, and she hadn't yet switched her lights on, she felt exactly as if a sun too fierce was dazzling her sight.

Johnny was standing there in the middle of her carpet ... Johnny whom she'd thought at the other side of the world. Big, fair, bulky Johnny, even broader than she remembered, and taller, in an American lightweight suit that was the last word in elegance, yet with that indefinable air of the outdoor man about him, so bronzed that his hair looked bleached. Johnny Carruthers, the bridge-builder, globe-trotter, probably here today and gone tomorrow. She'd become used to life without him. Why had he come back? But she wouldn't allow him to shatter her complacency, to disturb her hard-won peace of mind.

None of this showed. She knew it didn't, and the knowledge gave her confidence.

'Oh, hullo, Johnny, surprise, surprise!' She held out a hand, his engulfed it, released it. 'How nice to see you,' she added.

Nice.

His eyes swept over her, widened in appreciation. He whistled.

'Can this be you?'

Not the most tactful thing to say.

'Why not, Johnny?'

He shrugged. 'Why not, indeed? Yes ... this new you

matches that voice I heard over the phone. It ought to have prepared me.'

She said, very evenly, 'It's not a new self to me, Johnny. It's one I've lived with for almost five years. It's been a very different life.'

His gaze was direct, his eyes, deeply blue, holding hers. He'd always been that way. 'You mean since Godfrey died?'

She caught her breath in slightly, then relaxed. He must never know that the greatest difference in her life, the biggest emptiness, had been that Johnny Carruthers hadn't been in it. Nor that she'd been a different person ever since Johnny had broken his heart over another woman and had roamed the world in an effort to forget.

So she said to his question, 'Yes, of course,' and turned away a little.

He caught her coppery sleeve, flared from the elbows.

'Henrietta, we don't have to avoid all mention of Godfrey, do we? I mean it wouldn't seem fair. He was so much part of our earlier life.'

She said smoothly, unresentfully, 'He's *still* part of *my* life.' She waved towards her mantelpiece. 'And so is his mother. She spends a holiday here with me every year. Godfrey has his place here with me.'

Johnny's expression was unreadable. 'Yes, but is it the right place?'

Henrietta stiffened. 'Johnny, it's not for you to tell me what place that is. Though I can't think what you mean.'

'Then I'll have to tell you, won't I? I mean there ought to be a happy medium. By now it ought not to be a case of shuttering your feelings when he's mentioned, nor ought he to be forgotten. Get me?'

'No. And I don't think I'll try to analyse. I'll simply tell you what the position is as far as I'm concerned. His picture is upon my mantelpiece. It always will be. But I don't shut myself away from life because of his memory. That's not healthy.'

Johnny was staring at her, a thick crease between his brows. 'I'd like to think you meant that.'

'I do. But let's leave it at that. I don't like to be taken to pieces, to have people wondering what goes on in my head. Thoughts should be private. Tell me what you've been doing, Johnny? Lately, I mean.'

'Building bridges in Arizona. I always wanted that. Very satisfying.'

Henrietta said, 'The big stuff. New Zealand will seem small beer after that, I suppose.' She said it slightly contemptuously.

Johnny grinned. Very hard, always, to make Johnny mad. 'No, I've gained the experience I thought I needed for New Zealand. I've come back to the most stimulating and challenging thing I've ever done ... I hope.'

'Where?'

'Sorry, it's confidential as yet.'

Henrietta nodded, not at all put out. 'I'm used to that sort of thing. Working in the Department, you get used to keeping your own counsel. Will this mean you'll stay? Or are you just consultant for this job?'

No one could have guessed from her tone how much his answer meant to her.

He said slowly, 'I could be home for good. Not in New Zealand, but in the South Pacific. Perhaps mainly in Australia, but I'll be here part of the time.'

Henrietta had a curious, hollow feeling. How odd. She'd felt hollow when he'd gone away five years ago, before Godfrey died. What was *this* hollowness due to? Her heart answered her. Because she was afraid. Afraid of caring again. *Again?* She'd never stopped caring. But he would never know. If you couldn't have what you wanted, at least you could keep your pride.

She said slowly, 'Yes, I can imagine you'd be in Australia more than here. There'd not be enough big jobs here to challenge you, would there?'

He snorted. 'Henrietta, darling! We are one of the

few places in the world with regions still largely unexplored, and a small population. As it grows we'll have to bring in our more remote areas—areas that with bridges to cross rivers and chasms would no longer be remote. Yes, there's enough of a challenge to keep me here altogether if I decide on that. And after all, it *is* my home.'

She said, 'Is it? Is it really? I mean you were born in Malaya, and your parents——'

'My parents left me here to strike New Zealand roots. They're coming back anyway, but to Auckland. Dad is retiring at last, says he's too old now for this travelling engineer game. I say, can't you get someone to stand in for you tonight? I can't think of anything I'd rather do than just spend the evening here.'

Henrietta frowned. 'That's a bit high-handed, surely. I mean even to expect it. My job is very important to me. It can't be relegated. It——'

His eyes were alight with laughter. 'Not even if you'd gone down suddenly with 'flu, or dysentery, say?'

Henrietta pulled a face at him. 'Idiot! Besides, I *want* to go.'

Johnny chuckled. 'You've never lost *that* habit, anyway ... pulling faces. Gosh, what a terror you were!' Then before she could say anything, he came across to her, took her elbows, turned her round to the faint light of the window and said: 'Yes, they are. It's the only description.'

Henrietta blinked. 'Description of what?'

'Your eyes. Peat-brown, that's what they are. First time I ever saw a stack of peat was on the Island of Mull, driving across it to get the ferry-boat to Iona. Outside a whitewashed cottage was a stack of peats. And I thought: that's exactly the colour of Henrietta's eyes. Blackish-brown. And hair to match.'

Henrietta said firmly, ignoring the compliment— Johnny had always been good at compliments—'Mull? Then you've been to Britain? I thought that was the only spot in the world you'd not visited. When were you there?'

He still had hold of her elbows. He looked down on her, his grip too tight for comfort. 'I arrived there two days after you flew back here from London Airport.'

Henrietta was taken off-guard momentarily. Regret washed over her. Oh, to have shared the magic of London with Johnny!

She recovered, said, 'Were you on business? Or were your people there?'

'I had business to see to.'

Of course, of course. He wouldn't have flown from India to London just to see one Henrietta King.

'How long were you there?'

'Six months. Long enough to lose my heart to Great Britain.'

Six months. Well, he hadn't flown back to New Zealand after that, he'd gone to the States, so his disappointment at missing her, if any, must have been very superficial.

She said, 'You lost your heart to Great Britain? Then why didn't you stay? Plenty of openings there for someone with your qualifications. You didn't have to come back.'

She felt the pressure of his hands. 'I told you I'd put down roots here. Just because I was born in Malaya and have wandered the world a bit doesn't mean I'm a displaced person. And I always get homesick sooner or later for Queenie and Pukewhetu.'

Queenie . . . Godfrey's mother. She had so beautifully mothered Henrietta and Johnny all through their lonely school holidays when their parents were usually so far away. Queenie, their fond nickname for Mrs. King.

Henrietta freed herself by saying, 'I must just check that my list is in my evening bag, though I think I have it word perfect. And Johnny Durant will be here in a moment and his friend Johnny McIntosh with him. We call him Jock, to distinguish between them. We'll have a sherry when they come.'

When she came back Johnny had Godfrey's photograph in his hands. He turned round and his eyes were too bright. Henrietta checked the answering rush of tears to her own eyes, but she felt the hard core of her self-control slipping. She mustn't let this crust round her heart melt. Of course Johnny had loved Godfrey. They both had.

Johnny said, 'You married him at his bedside, didn't you? Was he well enough to enter into the spirit of it? Was it a happy day for him? Or did he know that——'

Henrietta said, 'He knew. But we thought he had a year or so, not that it was to be just a matter of weeks.' Then she said, rather fiercely, 'But I'm still glad we had even those few weeks. Furnishing a flat in town ... pretending it was for longer.'

Johnny bent swiftly down and picked up a rose-petal that had fallen on to her lambskin rug and dropped it into the grate. When he straightened up he said, 'Sorry, Henrietta, I ought not to be recalling this to you, when you've got a function ahead of you—I suppose you have to appear just like any other blithe young girl ... people will never guess.'

Henrietta managed a smile. 'Oh, most of the External Affairs crowd know. They call me the Merry Widow.'

Her thoughts were sombre. A widow, yes, but she had never been a wife. Godfrey, although he had planned every detail with her, had never seen that furnished flat. There had been a wedding ceremony, certainly, but not a marriage. Godfrey had died in his sleep one night, smiling, as if he had glimpsed something happy.

Queenie had been wonderful; she had said to Henrietta, 'Thank you for making my lad so happy. It was very big of you, Henrietta.'

Startled at her choice of words, Henrietta had turned to her. 'Big of me, Queenie? But, Queenie, I *loved* Godfrey.'

Queenie, dry-eyed because her grief, a mother's grief, was too deep for tears, had said simply, 'Oh, Henrietta,

I always knew. It was always Johnny with you, wasn't it? Only——'

Henrietta had said, 'Only Johnny didn't want me, and Godfrey did. And the memory of Godfrey will always be my sheet-anchor, Queenie.'

She tore her thoughts back to what Johnny was saying. He said, 'I'm glad you've earned the nickname of "merry". I wouldn't like to think that all that gaiety and liveliness and capacity for enjoying living had been quenched by Godfrey's death.'

At that moment the bell rang and John and Jock came in. If John was surprised that Henrietta called him Johnny when she introduced him to this bronzed stranger, he put it down to absentmindedness, muddling the two of them. This man, he realized, was the original of one of the photos on Henrietta's mantelpiece—a man poised on a crag with the horns of a thar sticking up over the peak above him. His eyes went across to it, but found it missing. He said nothing. There had been something in Henrietta's voice when she rang him. Something he'd never heard there before, a young and breathless something.

Henrietta was a good scout; look at the trouble she had taken with his fiancée, coaching her for the role she'd have to play when she was his wife; Julie had been scared stiff at the idea, but not any more, thanks to Henrietta.

Henrietta felt slightly enraged because Johnny had the nerve to play host, just as if he had the right. He went out to the kitchen and rummaged round for a packet of crisps. He looked through her filmy curtains to the scene that was deepening into night now, with lights blossoming goldenly among the trees. He caught her arm, drew her out on to the balcony of her fire-escape, said, 'Isn't it marvellous? Here you are, in the heart of town, yet you can look down into a pocket of native bush, preserved as a garden, even tree-ferns. Imagine a capital city, yet everywhere evidences of the

16

fact that less than two centuries ago this was virgin forest.'

Something caught at Henrietta's heartstrings. These were the things Johnny had always said, the dear, kindred things. But when he had gone a-wooing he hadn't looked for kinship, for comradeship. He'd fallen for empty prettiness and frilly femininity. Ah, pah!

She saw the lights of a car sweep up the hill, stop outside, back to a perfect position beside her gate.

She said firmly, 'There's the official car and punctuality is a necessary virtue in our kind of work. Johnny and Jock will be ready to go.'

Johnny said quickly, 'Is this a fairly big show? I mean crowds of people where one more or less would be unnoticed? I mean, no one will be announced, will they? How about me coming too?'

Henrietta looked completely horrified. 'You'll do nothing of the sort. I wouldn't know what to do with you. No gate-crashing friends allowed. Johnny, you'll have to go. Come round tomorrow—and I mean tomorrow night. I'm on duty all day, at the office and outside it.'

She took the crisps from him, put them on a shelf. 'We didn't need them anyway.'

He shrugged. 'I know. I just wanted you on your own to ask you if I might come.'

Henrietta said, 'Well, praise the saints you had enough sense not to ask in front of them.'

'Why?'

Her eyelids flickered. (Because they'd have said, 'Of course come along. You'd never stand out as a stranger in that throng.')

Instead she said firmly, 'Because they would think I had very odd friends. Come on.'

The other two men wasted no time in getting out of the flat.

Henrietta said, 'Johnny can't understand our on-the-dot timing. He's been in Arizona building bridges and the minutes don't count. And just because he's known me since I wore hockey boots and a brace on my teeth, he thinks he can disrupt my schedule.'

Johnny sounded quite stirred. 'Brace on your teeth! You never wore a brace on your teeth! Your teeth were perfect. Don't I know it? Wasn't Queenie always hounding Godfrey and me back to the bathroom and telling us to take as long over our brushing as you did?'

Henrietta chuckled. 'Just a saying. Haven't you noticed that in every story where the girl marries the one-time boy next door, they say he'd known her since she had buck teeth?'

Johnny looked at the swirls and layers of her high-piled hair and said, 'Well, I've known you since you had an Eton crop. That must have taken some growing.'

She looked at him pityingly. 'Poor man from the waybacks! He's never heard of a switch, obviously. This all comes apart, dear man, so I can sleep in comfort.'

The function had been in progress an hour when she saw him come in. There was no hesitancy about him. In fact he strode in with the air of making up time for being unavoidably late. He'd changed into correct kit, and was weaving his way through the groups as if he was a man with a purpose and knew where he was going. What effrontery! Then she lost him.

It was quite a few minutes before she saw him again. She missed the drift of what her guest was saying, saw Johnny stop, take a glass from a tray, smile at the waitress, scoop up a savoury and continue on to stop on the fringe of a group into which, naturally, being Johnny, he was received immediately.

Henrietta said quickly, 'I'm sorry, do excuse me. I just caught sight of someone from Arizona ... but he's evidently met up with a crowd he knows, so I don't have to worry about him. Yes, it's an early luncheon, twelve sharp, so we can get away on the sight-seeing. I do hope we'll have a day like today, so much more

18

enjoyable when there's no wind. We're having a scenic drive all round the heights of Wellington, then out a little distance up the coast road. Yes, I certainly do think the wives of the delegates deserve this ... they don't see much of their husbands and not everyone wants to fill in the time shopping. Yes, there'll be a courier on every bus to point out places of historic interest and answer questions. In fact, I'm one myself.'

'In fact,' said Johnny's voice at her elbow, 'I'm another. I've just got myself a job. Jock McIntosh roped me in. He said they don't want to risk you having another go of laryngitis such as you had two weeks ago, so I'm to spell you. How about a few introductions, Henrietta?'

She dared not show her fury in front of these charming people. Nobody, except Johnny, would have known that inwardly she was seething.

Apparently no one thought it strange that a bridge-builder, newly in from Arizona, should be here with the Trade Mission. They probably thought he had steel interests. In company with Henrietta he chatted easily with oil magnates, journalists, wool buyers from Yorkshire and Japan, textile designers, advertising men, greater and lesser lights among the secretaries, made himself charming to the wives and altogether it kept Henrietta in a state of great apprehension.

She knew only too well that in this sort of mood Johnny could attempt anything. He hadn't changed. He was still ripe for mischief, his eyes dancing with devilment every time they met hers, and just brimming with controlled laughter. As long as that control did not slip!

She said to him desperately when for once they found themselves isolated, 'Johnny, I beg you, I implore you ... don't go too far. If you see the Prime Minister or any of the Cabinet bearing down on any group we happen to be in, make yourself scarce, *please*?'

His well-cut mouth twitched in the old familiar way. 'Oh, not to worry, Henrietta my darling, I've already had a chat with the P.M. He recognized me, strange as it may seem. He turned up on the job I was on in the States last time he was over to visit the President. I was introduced as a fellow-Kiwi. And I had a word with the Minister of Public Works too, but then I saw him yesterday . . . about my hush-hush job.'

Henrietta was bereft of speech for a moment. Then she said, 'They—they didn't ask how you came to be here?'

He looked at her with mock reproach. 'Come, come, they're much too nice to do a thing like that. Not like you . . . you're doing your best to make me feel a gate-crasher.'

'As if you aren't exactly that,' said Henrietta bitterly. 'All right, Johnny, you've had your fun. Now go.'

'Not likely. Don't you know I never give up till I get what I want?'

Her eyes flickered up to his. 'I know you're persistent, even contrary to the point of being cussed, Johnny, but you don't *always* get what you want, you know. And excuse me . . . that woman over there on the fringe of that lot looks lonely. One of the shy ones perhaps, who'd rather have married a man who lived in dull, happy obscurity. But they're so sweet.'

She moved off, but Johnny kept pace with her. 'I'll buttress you, Henrietta. Then when you see someone else in need, I'll stay with this one. I like these gallant souls who'd rather be home knitting for their grandchildren. Who knows, I might even make her evening for her. "Bronzed hero from the outposts of civilization who stayed with me all evening. And there were such ravishing girls there too." Can't you imagine her letter to her daughter running on those lines?'

Henrietta gave up. Johnny was just too, too awful.

It was inevitable, of course, that he should take her home. If you could call it that, since it was in one of the cars provided by the Department.

She said, but without hope, 'You mustn't come in,

Johnny. I'm tired.'

He said, with a sudden descent into seriousness and an air as if he really cared, 'I know. And no wonder. But it's the sort of tiredness that won't let you sleep. You're wound up, you need to relax. I'm coming in. I'll make you unwind.'

She stopped dead on the stairs, heaved a sigh. 'Since when have *you* been considered relaxing, Johnny?'

He grinned. 'That's a point. We usually strike sparks off each other, don't we? But maybe I've changed. You might let me try, anyway.'

'Have I any choice? Could I stop you if I wanted to?'

Again the grin. 'The answer to both questions is no. I won't have you going on as if I were practically a stranger.'

She said slowly, 'After five years, most people would be strangers.'

'Yes, most, but not you and me.'

Surprisingly, she accepted that. 'No, that's true,' but spoilt it by adding, 'After all, brothers and sisters sometimes don't meet for years.'

She tried to look away from him, but seemingly he had still the old compelling quality and she had to meet that blue gaze.

He pulled a mouth, in mock anger, and said, 'That's too damn silly for words, so we'll regard it as unsaid.'

Henrietta went ahead, unlocked the door.

Johnny's hand closed over her wrist. They measured glances.

He said, 'One doesn't propose to one's sister, you know.'

Henrietta felt a little pulse flutter at the hollow of her throat and hoped it wouldn't show, but his eyes were on her face.

She said coolly, 'Could you call that a proposal—that letter you wrote nearly four years ago?'

A derisive note crisped his voice. 'I think it would stand up as just that in a court of inquiry. It was there in black and white, asking you to marry me.'

Derision edged her voice too. 'Exactly. The letter of the law, if not of the spirit. Set out like a business proposition.'

A gleam shot into his eye. His grip on her wrist tightened.

'Well, it's quite evident that I'm not much good at conveying undying love in a letter. I didn't even rate an answer. But now I'm here, perhaps——'

With a swift movement she freed herself and stepped back, locking her hands behind her. 'No, Johnny. Oh, no. Don't try to put that one over. You're wasting your time. I've changed in many ways, but in one I've remained the same. I think the only possible basis for marriage is love.'

He remained where he was, very still, very erect. Then he said slowly, 'Then it wasn't out of pity that you married Godfrey?' She turned a little white and he said quickly, 'Oh, Henrietta, forgive me. I'd no right to say that. Only I did wonder. He was ill so soon after. Oh hell, I'm making a mess of things as usual.'

But she'd gained control of her feelings and said very gently, 'Johnny, I expect it was because you were away at the time. You remember you went off to Singapore when Deirdre and you parted. So your timing is all wrong. Godfrey asked me to marry him *before* he knew he had leukaemia.'

She wasn't looking at him now. She just heard him say, rather quietly for the ebullient Johnny, 'Oh. Well, naturally I'd wondered. It was so soon after the news of your engagement that I heard he was desperately ill.'

Henrietta bent to switch a wall heater on. 'It's gone a little chilly.'

With a swift movement he crossed, switched it off, then went across to the fireplace, lifted a box of matches from the mantel and said, bending to her set fire, 'I like the look of an open fire, and don't say: "You won't be staying long," because I am. We have more than five years to catch up on.'

Henrietta said slowly, 'We can't catch up on them, Johnny. There are some things even an engineer can't bridge.'

His jaw set. 'I've never yet failed to bridge a river—or a chasm.'

There was quite a silence. This in itself was remarkable to him. The old Henrietta had been quick, sometimes too quick, with her answers.

Then she said, as if she'd been weighing it up, 'There are bigger things than chasms, than rivers. You don't bridge oceans, for instance.'

His own reply was prompt. 'Not with steel girders, perhaps. But oceans no longer divide. Air-travel spans them in hours. Look, Henrietta, you were for ever dipping into Madame Beaudonais's scrapbooks. Didn't you ever read that clipping about the Atlantic?—Oh, I can see you don't remember it. Odd, I'd have thought you would have, because as kids we were always so conscious of the seas that separated our parents from us. It was only a fragment. The two lines I liked were:

*'Once between us lay the Atlantic
... yet I felt your hand in mine.'*

'Now do you remember? And get my meaning?'

The peaty-brown eyes met the vivid blue ones. 'I remember it, Johnny. It's not a good choice for you. The next two lines went:

*'Now I feel your hand in mine,
... yet between us the Atlantic.'*

'And it wasn't a clipping. It was in Madame's writing. She'd heard it on the radio. She didn't even know who'd written it.'

Johnny picked up her hand, lying between them on the couch, and said, 'But I'm here and your hand is in mine and there's no Atlantic—even a symbolic one—rolling between us, is there?'

Henrietta said crossly, 'Of all the daft conversations! What sort of an answer could any girl make to that? Johnny, what will you have? Tea or coffee?'

He laughed in the most maddening fashion. 'You've answered me all right. Tea, thanks. A good big pot of tea.'

Henrietta got up, thankful to have something to do. 'Just a biscuit with it?'

Johnny said, 'No fear. What have you got in your fridge? I missed out on a good many of the eats tonight. Jock said they'd handed round some delicious chicken curry earlier. I'll have a mixed grill, thanks.'

Henrietta helped him cook it in a daze. If anyone had told her, just this morning, that at eleven at night she'd be sitting opposite Johnny at her little round table, eating lamb chops, eggs and tomatoes, to say nothing of indigestible and fattening fried bread, she'd have thought they were mad.

'That's good,' said Johnny, picking up a bone in his fingers, 'you're warming up. Can't look like a tragedy queen for ever, you know.'

Henrietta lost her coolness completely. 'Oh, Johnny, shut up! I've never looked like a tragedy queen. I've too much sense of humour. I've told you I've had a lot of fun these last few years.'

'I believe you have.' He wiped his fingers and lips on a napkin. 'But was it our kind of fun?'

'No, perhaps not. Ours was crude, boisterous fun. But this has done something for me, just the same. Now, let's wash the dishes. I can't stand getting up to dirty dishes on a working morning.'

But even after they were washed he wouldn't go.

They sat down again in front of the fire. He asked after everyone in the Dragonshill district, the Beaudonais family, the Llewellyns, the Greenwoods, the Richards.

Henrietta felt her alarms of the earlier part of the evening subsiding. This was all very natural. But she was wary and did not mention that she was giving this up and returning to Dragonshill and Pukewhetu.

She'd rather keep on this friendly, light footing, with none of the meaningful sparring that stabbed at her so. Johnny would go off to whatever project he'd come here for and she would go down South and most of his time would be spent in Australia in all probability.

She looked up at him quite frankly. 'This is better, Johnny. Back on the old friendly footing. Look, let's wipe out all remembrance of that letter. It spoiled our relationship. Made us self-conscious with each other. Our links all lie in our earlier years. I like it best that way. The intervening years are best forgotten. Okay?'

He grunted, stirred. 'Where's your bathroom, Henrietta? Through that door?'

She nodded. 'The guest-towel rack is the one behind the door.'

He came back, sat himself down rather carefully, turned to her, and before she could wonder what he was up to, seized her in a grip she knew she'd have no chance of breaking. It pinned her against the back of the couch.

His eyes danced. And the next moment the horrible, wet, cold feel of a suddenly applied face-cloth made her flinch.

She couldn't do more than squawk a protest because she didn't want soap and water in her mouth. She had to close her eyes too.

He was very thorough. Then he fired the face-cloth on to the hearth-tiles, snatched his handkerchief out of his pocket and effectively silenced her indignant splutterings by drying her face as thoroughly as he had washed it.

Then he said calmly, 'It's okay ... I'm not agin make-up ... it was very charmingly done, Henrietta, I only wanted to make quite sure they were still there.'

Glaring, she said between her teeth, 'What were still there?'

He chuckled. 'Your freckles. And they are. Not nearly as prominent as they used to be, but still there,

25

thank goodness. If you'd lost them, Freckle-face, I wouldn't have dared kiss you.'

And kiss her he did. Very efficiently. And was so long about it Henrietta couldn't keep struggling.

He lifted his head, looked down on her, still held against him, and said, smiling, 'Ah!' in a tone of the greatest satisfaction.

Henrietta struggled up, said furiously, 'What do you mean? ... *Ah!*'

He shrugged. 'I mean there's no Atlantic between us. Or anything.'

She was so cross she got to her feet, rather inelegantly, stamped her foot and said: 'Of all the vanity! Just because I was too breathless to resist you, you took my—my—my impassiveness for response! Ohhhhhhhhh!' She actually gritted her teeth at him.

He gave way to mirth. 'You didn't want to resist, my darling Henrietta!'

She said, as calmly as she could, 'You are going. You are going right now!'

'Too right I am. Anything else—after a kiss like that—would be an anti-climax. Don't bother to see me out, sweetheart. I'll slam your downstairs door behind me.'

Still laughing, he stepped out into the passage, turned, sketched a mocking bow and said, 'See you at the bus depot at one-fifteen, Henrietta. Night-night. Sleep well.'

And Johnny Carruthers went running lightly, for all his bulk, down her stairs, whistling!

Shaken, unsure of herself, and furious, Henrietta retired to bed. And she knew she wouldn't sleep. A thousand thoughts would jangle through her mind ... details of tomorrow's doings, things she mustn't forget ... memories of yesteryears, would crowd in upon her, the old, bitter memories she would rather forget, the sweet ones she dared not remember. Oh, damn Johnny Carruthers! If only he'd stayed in Arizona! Or somewhere else not New Zealand! Why couldn't other engineers build this New Zealand bridge that was so hush-hush? Henrietta wanted to cling to this pseudo-contentment she'd built up for herself...she didn't want to be disturbed again. It wasn't fair to re-awaken the old longings.

She tried to read, first a romance, then a mystery, to try to distract her mind, but couldn't, and tossed and turned after she put her light off. How interminable the hours till morning were going to be! But suddenly she went out like a light, into a world of dreaming where the impossible became reality ... a world of two ... Johnny and Henrietta, a world where Deirdre and Godfrey had never existed.

CHAPTER TWO

HENRIETTA was amazed at how good a courier Johnny made. He'd always been knowledgeable about local history, both Maori and *pakeha*, but that had been of the places he'd lived in. Round Timaru where he'd been at boarding school, and the high country where he and Henrietta had spent almost every vacation with Godfrey and his people, at Pukewhetu ... the Hill of the Stars.

But she hadn't expected him to know so much about Wellington and the Paekakariki road that skirted the west coast of the North Island. She was even conscious of a slight feeling of chagrin—he knew more than she did, she might as well admit it.

The wives of the delegates were charming, light-hearted and prepared to love everything they saw, and there was no doubt they were enjoying having this personable male as their courier. Henrietta felt her resentment slipping away and told herself she must not fall under that undoubted charm again.

She tried to shake him off when the tour was over, but it was no use. She found herself making dinner for him back at the flat, after having turned down his offer to take her out for a meal. But she was not spending the evening with him again. Oh, no, not after last night.

Yet in spite of herself she found herself preparing the food he like best. Potato patties, not chips, with his steak, a Dutch sauce, piquant with lemon juice, on the shelled broad beans, and an open apple tart, spiced with cinnamon and with chopped and beaten dates mixed into the fruit pulp.

Over coffee Johnny said, waving a hand at the walls ... 'You like this life, Henrietta? Flat life? Can't somehow reconcile the old Henrietta with it. You belonged to the open spaces, to the mountains. I can see you now, careering along in the wind, on Dandy. Or skiing down the Hill of the Stars or out snow-raking with the men and as good as they were, freeing the sheep.

'But here ... only window-boxes for flowers, and a tub of geraniums on a fire-escape. And chimneys and multi-storey buildings on the skyline instead of the peaks of the Alps ... it just isn't you.'

She said slowly, 'It's not the Henrietta you knew years ago, Johnny. But this life has a fascination all its own. You may not realize how rewarding it is. You have a sense of helping your country—not in any spectacular way, of course, but by smoothing the paths for overseas people—people important to New Zealand.

'After all, half our Members of Parliament, including the P.M., must be farmers. They, too, long to get away from the city, from the pressure of it all, the often senseless criticism, the wear and tear upon the nerves, to the quietness of their acres. But they spend the greater part of their lives here in the Capital. It's no good you looking for that heedless tomboy of other years, Johnny. I'm twenty-nine, I've been married and widowed, and perhaps my needs of long ago are different now.'

'Then why,' he said, and his voice was harsh, 'are you returning to Dragonshill?'

She was shocked into silence.

After a while he said, 'There's no answer to that, is there? Why are you trying so hard to make me believe you've changed?'

There was no answer to that either, so she ignored it and said, 'How did you know I was going back? And why didn't you tell me you knew?'

'Because I was most intrigued to find out the reason why you didn't tell me. You're going to be there by Christmas, aren't you? Just a month away. Wouldn't it have been natural in the first few moments of my arrival to say, "Glad you came when you did, because you'd have missed me otherwise. I'm going home next month." But no. You kept silent. Why?'

(Why indeed? Because she had so passionately wanted him to think her very different from that long-ago Henrietta, who had idolized Johnny Carruthers. Who had been vulnerable, idealistic, always stupidly certain that her future was bound up with his. Till that disastrous spring when Deirdre Seelby had come into their lives. Well, it had worked, Johnny had seen her calm, confident, fitting easily into this semi-diplomatic world, well-groomed, attractive to other men. He hadn't missed any of the moves that that persistent attaché from one of the embassies had made to her; she'd realized that. And it had certainly piqued Johnny's interest. Henrietta decided she didn't like such men ... the ones who only recognized you as an attractive woman because other men obviously did.)

Johnny said, undisguised irritation in his voice, 'All right, all right. You don't have to go off into a day-dream. Answer me!'

She looked at him consideringly in what she knew was an aggravating way, then said mildly, 'I was thinking it out, wondering why I said nothing to you. Perhaps it was just that I thought you were here today and gone tomorrow and we'd not be seeing you at Dragons-hill. Anyway, how did you find out?'

'Well, I flew in to Christchurch Airport when I came to New Zealand. So I went down home for a fortnight.'

'What? A fortnight? But—but I had a letter from Queenie just last week and she didn't say a word. And one from Penny Beaudonais-Smith too. I——'

His eyes were expressionless, and that was unusual. 'They said nowt because I asked them to say nowt.'

'Why? I mean *you're* hauling *me* over the coals because I kept quiet about my plans, yet *you've* been holding out on *me*! Why, I ask you, why?'

He grinned a lazy sort of grin. 'Bit childish, perhaps, but I like to give people surprises. Remember? A much more simple reason than yours, for secretiveness.'

It didn't provoke her into explanations, which, no doubt, he hoped to do.

So presently he said, 'Penny and Hilary are very thrilled you're going. The great hazard with governesses at Dragonshill is that they can't take the loneliness. But you're used to it, and love it. And you're better qualified than most too, though I'd have thought, if you were wanting to get back into teaching, that any High School would have been open to you.

She said slowly, 'It wasn't particularly that I had a yen to get back into teaching, even though I love it. It——'

A satisfied gleam shot into his eye. 'But you're longing to get back to the mountains. To the solitudes. The lonely places of the earth.'

Henrietta knew an instant wariness. He wanted to think she did. Deirdre, whom he had idealized that unhappy spring of years ago, had given him up because she couldn't take the sort of life he was going to lead, in the solitary, dangerous and tough spots of the world. Later, he'd thought Henrietta was the one who could take it. *Nice* to be thought so suitable! Like weeding out applicants for a position. A very thrilling concept of marriage! He still thought there was a chance, did he? And for the same reasons!

She said, 'I think you've got it wrong, Johnny. It's merely a matter of gratitude and of feeling I could do a good job up there, for the people who did so much for me when I was a lonely, lost kid. They've had quite a time of it up at Dragonshill. Madame, as you know, is one hundred years old. She takes more looking after than she did, even though she's so wonderful for her age. Penny knows that any time now she could be confined to nursing her, with help from Hilary, of course, but they'd never be able to manage those two big houses, the shearing and mustering cooking as well as correspondence lessons.

'It would give them such peace of mind if, for say the

next three or four years, I was there for the schoolroom work. They know I can take the solitude and I'm not quite the same risk, marriage-wise, as the others. You know how it's always been ... the governesses marry the shepherds and when their own babies are coming move nearer civilization and doctors—with no temperamental river to rage in flood between them and the road.'

Johnny said, 'Do you mean you consider yourself a cut above shepherds these days?'

She did not let this provoke her. She said calmly, 'That's too ridiculous to answer.'

'Then you must mean marriage has no place in your scheme of things ... in your own future.'

'Just that,' said Henrietta lightly.

He was angry. 'I've never heard such rubbish! Emotionally, life ought not to be over for you. Do you mean to say that those few weeks as Godfrey's wife satisfied you for the rest of your life? It's perfectly ridiculous. It wastes all your home-making talents, wastes all the wealth of affection ... in fact of passion ... that you're capable of.'

It made Henrietta feel breathless. She got up. 'We must wash these dishes. I have to be out at seven-fifteen.'

He said, 'Where? What's on? I'll——'

Her lips twitched. 'You just can't gate-crash in on this, John Carruthers. You wouldn't be in the least welcome.'

'You mean I'd be gooseberry? An unwelcome third? All right. I won't push in. But where are you going, and with whom?'

Henrietta shook her head at him. 'Oh, Johnny, Johnny! As if I'd tell you. Once bitten twice shy! You'd think of some reason for turning up.'

He was not set back, said, grinning, 'Okay. But skip all the other engagements while I'm here, won't you? It's natural for me to spend most of the time I'm in Wellington with you. You're the only bit of family I've got here.'

Henrietta wouldn't have dared say she was baby-sitting for Jock and Rhona. It would have meant another night sitting alone and near. Another night of questions and answers, perhaps of revelations. She knew exactly what she was going to do.

After they had washed up she said lightly, 'Amuse yourself with a book now, won't you, Johnny? There's the latest *Weekly News*. An exceptionally good column by Grammaticus this week. You'll love it—Greek and Roman history. And my library book is a whodunit. If you haven't read it you can take it back with you to your hotel if you like.'

They measured glances. Johnny said, 'Thanks all the same, but I'll read it here. I'll still be around when you get back.'

Henrietta very much doubted that and checked a grin. She said, 'You take a lot for granted, Johnny. Who's to know that wouldn't prove very embarrassing?'

He got the point. 'Oh, bringing someone back, are you? Sounds to me as if you need chaperoning, my lass.'

She laughed outright. 'I don't see you as a duenna!'

His eyes danced. 'Nor would anyone else if they'd seen us last night. Kissing, I mean. Kissing like that!'

Henrietta was furious with herself for blushing. Johnny seized her by the arms and looked delighted. 'Good show ... you still blush. This is really something. I've been back only twenty-four hours and already you're losing your icy disdain. Thank heaven, I've no use for snow-maidens.'

Henrietta freed herself with one swift movement and said over her shoulder, 'I must get ready. It will take some time. Settle down with Agatha Christie, will you, Johnny Carruthers?'

Her eyes were dancing as she surveyed herself in the mirror. Johnny was not, for once, going to have it his way. He'd expect her to emerge in an evening frock the way she'd spoken, or at least dressed for the theatre. She wouldn't even bother to change. This cream crimplene frock with the simple round neck with a long string of brown beads over it would do for to-night and she could drive back here tomorrow to change for church.

Her overnight bag was ready except for her make-up kit. It was beautifully hot so she wouldn't even need a cardigan. Thank goodness her bedroom door led out to the tiny back hall and she could slip into the kitchen-ette and down the fire-escape.

On a sudden impulse she went across to her dressing-table, pulled open a drawer, took out a box of gloves and from under it drew out a letter, creased and old. She slipped it into her bag. She went very quietly, though no doubt if Johnny heard her go through he'd think nothing of it. She opened the door silently, and stepped out on to the balcony.

The fire-escape was one of the iron ladder variety and it ended a fair distance from the ground, but that didn't worry Henrietta. Her bag had a long strap, so she hung it round her neck and went swiftly down. She hoped no one saw her and took her for an escaping thief. She dropped lightly on to a strip of lawn on the edge of the bush Johnny had admired last night, sped round to her garage and backed her Mini out.

Just before she reached Jock's house, she stopped at a telephone booth and rang her own number.

She had to subdue a wild giggle at Johnny's surprise when she said, 'Henrietta here,' and he replied promptly: 'What? What can you mean: "Henrietta here"? She's in her bedroom. Oh ... sorry, I get it. You're another Henrietta. By heck, you're not ... Hen-rietta, that's *your* voice. What the——'

'Give me a chance to speak, you poor confused man. Listen ... I wasn't going to risk any more gate-crashing. I slipped down the fire-escape. Would you be sure to lock that door for me when you leave, Johnny? It's not safe to leave it. You'll find a piece of Pavlova cake in the green tin in the cupboard beside the fridge. It's already filled with cream and fruit. And there are plenty of biscuits.'

He said firmly, 'I'll be here when you get home and you can thank your lucky stars I'm a civilized sort of chap and don't give you the spanking you deserve. Of all the dirty tr——'

She interrupted to say sweetly: 'I won't be home. I'm spending the night with friends. I'll see you some time next week then, not before. Johnny, you ought not to ... you can get prosecuted for using language like that over the phone. Bye-bye.'

She giggled the rest of the way to Jock's. It made her feel much better.

Henrietta read small William and Elizabeth McIntosh a bedtime story based on the rewards of always telling the truth and behaving kindly to people and virtue winning the day, and decided she was an out-and-out hypocrite.

As she crawled upstairs in the wake of the children, pretending she was a great, big, growly, teddy-bear, she was pleased to find herself thinking this. 'That's good,' she said to herself, 'see the funny side of it, Henrietta! Don't take any of it too seriously. There was enough heartache and longing years ago. Don't let Johnny Carruthers disturb you ever again.'

But when, half an hour later, she stole up to see if the pair of them were asleep and covered, she found she was still vulnerable. Impossible not to feel a pang for all you had not known when you looked down on sleeping children ... William was a large child, fair ... Johnny Carruthers's son would look like this. Henrietta ran away from her thoughts and went downstairs. But she succumbed, after all, to the temptation of reading that letter over once more.

The date was four years old. She hadn't seen Johnny for over a year when it arrived, not since he'd gone to Singapore. She'd wondered at the lack of letters till then. Johnny had always been a good correspondent, with a vivid pen. But when Deirdre had broken off their engagement it had knocked him badly.

There had been a brief note of congratulation to the two of them when she had become engaged to Godfrey, and a terse, agonized one when Godfrey had died ... because Johnny had lost his best friend. Then nothing more till this, though he wrote to Queenie and Mike King regularly.

Although she knew it by heart she picked it up and read it. It was a good idea ... it might serve to stiffen her against the charm of John Carruthers.

'Dear Henrietta,
The time I set myself has gone. It's more than a year now since Godfrey died and I know he'd not have expected life to cease, emotionally, for you because we had lost him.

I expected to be able to fly to New Zealand to put this to you in person, but though I was due for three months' leave after finishing the job in Thailand, something else has cropped up and I'm in Alaska for a month, and am facing two months in Manitoba before going on to join Dad at the job in the Argentine.

I know you'll understand my position ... even if some women wouldn't ... because of your own background, and your parents always going from pillar to post and back again. One is at the call of the job and it holds up so many other folk and the delays cost countries a mint of money—so I've no show now of making it.

So it has to be by letter. I won't talk about Godfrey. Not in a letter. It still hurts too much. Or about other things. So I'll get to the point as I can't stand havering. You're a sensible girl and will see it the right way, I know.

We both know I can't offer you anything but second-best, but I'm sure we could make a go of it.

36

We know each other so well, and I feel you'd enjoy this kind of life immensely. You'd see places right off the normal tourist beat. I'll try, if humanly possible, to get enough time to come for you, but if not, how about flying over to wherever I am, to marry me?

Heavens, what a life! I suppose Alaska sounds remote and reasonably peaceful, but I've just had an urgent call to go to New York. I can't even finish this letter. Will it do, just like this? Knowing you, I'm sure of your understanding. I've exactly half an hour to leave instructions, get packed and airborne. But I'll be looking for a quick answer, girl, to this address. Especially as I can now post this from New York.

Yours, ever as aye,

Johnny.'

As always when she read it, only a few words made any impact ... 'We both know I can't offer you anything but second-best ...' So Deirdre still had her place in his heart. Or had then. And then, or now, Henrietta would never settle for any man's second-best. She had too warm a nature, she loved Johnny too well. Less than a full giving, from him to her, would turn her love sour. It had been unthinkable then. It still was.

She had not trusted herself to write. She had cabled Alaska.

Merely: 'Sorry unable even consider the proposition stop wish you well in all your engineering prospects stop regards Henrietta.'

And from that day to this there had never been a word from him. She had had to rely on the occasional scraps of news from Queenie and Uncle Mike.

A scrap of paper had fallen out of the letter, a typed poem. She had copied it from one of Madame's scrapbooks, a poem of World War Two that had fitted Henrietta's own love story so aptly—at least two verses of it. Irresistibly she read it again. An Australian poet, one C. McEwen of New South Wales, had written to a

37

lad in khaki:

> *'Oh, who shall sing the Summer in*
> *Now Johnny is away?*
> *There's none can whistle down the wind*
> *So blithe and wild and gay——*
> *Sweet tangled tunes more golden than*
> *The first gold Summer day!*
>
> *So, who shall sing my Summer in*
> *Since wild seas part us twain?*
> *Oh, sorrowing! The days may come*
> *In gold and wind and rain,*
> *There's none can sing my Summer in*
> *Till Johnny's home again!'*

Henrietta's eyes were full of unshed tears as she gazed down at the words. Summer was here ... almost. In two days' time it would be December. And the tussock and snowgrass would be blowing gold about Dragonshill. And she would be there. And Johnny would be here in Wellington, with Cook Strait between them. But for how long? Certainly Australia was nearer than Alaska or Arizona, but even so, Dragonshill was so remote, so difficult of access with its unbridged river, the Pawerawera, the River of Dread, that they could not expect to see him there very often. A wild regret washed over Henrietta. She wished she hadn't consented to return to Dragonshill.

Wellington was the heart of New Zealand. All ways led to it, road, sea, air. And if Johnny was consultant engineer for some big bridge project, he'd have to be here often discussing details with officials of the Government. It could have been rather—wonderful, even if there was no future in it. A bitter-sweet pleasure, but—but better than not having him at all.

Henrietta said to herself: 'You fool! You utter fool! Not again, Henrietta, not again. You were all his for the taking, those long years ago, and he never noticed you in that way. You had to watch Deirdre come into his life to see love wakening in him, and awareness ... you had to watch her sweep him off his feet, then drop him because she wouldn't take his sort of life. And now, because a man needs a wife *and* because he thinks you're made of the right stuff, he wants you to wed him. He'll even play round with a little lovemaking like the other night to fool you—and perhaps himself —into thinking we're in love. Oh, pah! Don't weaken, Henrietta, don't be spineless. You want all or nothing from Johnny Carruthers.' She didn't sleep well.

When she entered the flat the next morning to change for church, there wasn't a sign of Johnny. The Pavlova had been eaten, certainly, and the cooky jar was depleted, but the dishes were washed and put away and even the Agatha Christie neatly tucked into the bookends where her library books belonged. Perhaps it was possible she had convinced him she did not want him. Again that curious hollowness took possession of Henrietta. She felt restless, longing for the phone to ring, to hear steps bounding up her stairs.

She got into a lightweight suit, harebell blue, with a short, loose top to it, fringed with ivory silk tassels, and slipped a pearl ring on one of the fingers of her right hand. She picked up pearl-embroidered ivory gloves, a handbag to match and a black morocco-bound hymn-book and set off, walking, for St. John's. It wasn't really far, downhill. And walking would be better. It might loosen up more than muscles.

The quiet mellowness and the cool of the interior of the church did more for her than the walking. She bent her head. The prayer she prayed wasn't the kind she usually prayed before a service, but she thought God understood most prayers, even rather selfish ones. It wasn't right, in a world of such want, such cruelty, a world that never seemed to be entirely free of war and rebellion, to pray: 'God, help me, please? I've adjusted to life without Johnny and I don't know how to handle this, or what I really want. I'll have to leave the future to you. Please show me the way. And now bless this service for all who come and are in any need whatever. Amen.'

She settled back on her seat, glanced briefly to her right, and found Johnny was beside her. His mouth was grave, his eyes twinkling. 'Good morning, Henrietta,' he whispered. 'Now you can't possibly be cross with me in church. It isn't ethical.'

It wasn't. She knew that. But she whispered back, 'It also isn't ethical to take advantage of that. It's not a reason for churchgoing.'

He shook his head at her. 'You're not the only reason I'm at church, even if you're the reason why I'm in *this* church. I promised Queenie before I left Pukewhetu that I'd never neglect churchgoing—or some kind of worship—even in outlandish places. I've worshipped in grass huts and tin sheds—and in tunnels under the earth, wherever we've been able to hold a service.' He smiled at her, a smile that loosened the tightness round her heart. 'I rang Jock, asked where you usually worshipped. He said you were a member here.'

At that moment they rose for the entry of the Bible, the minister, the choir.

After the service he said to her, 'You aren't cooking for me today. You're coming to my hotel for lunch, I told them I'd probably have a guest. Then we're going a really long drive—to Wanganui.'

In response to her raised eyebrows he said, 'I know it's a fair step, a hundred and twenty-six miles each way, but it won't matter if we're late back. It will be cooler then, anyway. After lunch we'll make a quick getaway, except that we'll drop in at your flat to get your swim-suit, if that suits you. Thought of a swim at Waikanae Beach on the way. How about that?'

Might as well, thought Henrietta, because having Johnny here was going to be brief.

'Good. Henrietta, I'd forgotten how lovely you look in blue. Not all brunettes do. That suit is perfect. And

I have something in my room for you that will be just right with it.'

His room was very high up and looked right down the harbour where, beyond the tall masts of the overseas shipping, pleasure yachts were tacking to and fro on a glittering, Prussian Blue tide. One of Wellington's sparkling, sea-tanged days. But if they stayed here, the roads to the bays would be jammed with traffic. They would be able to relax more in Wanganui. Henrietta felt contentment seeping into her ... which was dangerous. She had let that service of worship penetrate her guard.

She stood looking out of the window and he opened a drawer and came across to her, holding a box he sprung open. She gave an involuntary cry of pleasure. Any girl would.

They were beautifully matched, a string of cultured pearls.

'From Japan,' said Johnny. 'I was there nine months.'

She said, touching a finger to the lustre of the pearls, 'But that's a long time ago. Queenie told me you were there. Did you keep them all this time?'

He looked at her sharply. 'I certainly didn't buy them for someone else, if that's what you mean, shrew! There have been only two women in my life ... Deirdre and you. And apart from the fact I didn't go to Japan till after our engagement was washed up, we weren't engaged long enough to buy presents like this. If you want the full story, I took them to London with me, thinking you were still a receptionist at New Zealand House. After all, my only news of you was also secondhand—through Queenie. Evidently you decided to come back to New Zealand very suddenly. I didn't get her letter saying you were on your way home, till I got to London. It was forwarded on.

'Bit of a let-down. Alone among all those millions to find your one link with home had left London forty-eight hours before that.'

Her tone was light. 'Yes, there's a great camaraderie among fellow-Kiwis in London. It would be disappointing for you.'

He looked at her, brows down. 'Given to understatement, aren't you? You didn't always have that reputation. Everything was twopence-coloured once.'

Her mouth was wry. 'Yes. All my geese were swans. I told you I'd changed—even if I haven't lost the freckles.'

Their eyes dropped to the pearls again. 'No rubbish about not being able to accept them, mind,' he warned. 'I won't stand for that.'

She said slowly, 'I'd love them. I love pearls, as you can see.' She waved her hand with its pearl ring at him. 'As long as I can take them from one old friend to any other, not——' she stopped, at a loss.

He said, rather harshly, 'I know what you were going to say. Not as a love-gift. That was it, wasn't it?'

She said cautiously, 'Well, sort of.'

For the first time Henrietta realized Johnny too had changed. She had never seen his eyes look really hard before.

He said, 'You mean taking it doesn't commit you to anything, don't you?'

She played it cool. 'I do. It has to be that way, Johnny. It's not fair otherwise. I don't think you men know how hard it is to be a woman. Sometimes one has to be—well, slightly ungracious—rather than run the risk of seeming to encourage. But as long as you understand that, I'll accept it and treasure it . . . for the days of auld lang syne.'

He accepted that. 'Right. Turn round. Let me put it on for you.'

Their eyes met in the mirror. Hers hastily disengaged. She could scarcely bear his touch. Odd how only one man had ever had this magic . . . this power to stir her.

He turned her round, surveyed her throat, said, 'Perfect.'

He took her hand ... examined the ring. 'Did God-frey buy that for you?'

The hand in his shook slightly. 'No. It's much older than anything Godfrey could have bought. Madame Beaudonais gave it to me. I felt it should go to Penny or Hilary for their children, but she—they—said Madame had so much jewellery to leave that they would like me to have this. I was very thrilled. It gave me a sense of belonging.'

'I'm glad it was Madame's. And that she gave it to you.'

Did he mean glad it wasn't Godfrey's gift? But that was absurd. There was nothing of that in his feeling for her. She mustn't look for such things.

He said, 'The old nostalgia ... does it still crop up, Henrietta? The longing to belong to some permanent place. A feeling we used to share when we were kids? And if only Godfrey hadn't died you would be at Pukewhetu because he would be farming it, not his younger brother—or perhaps they would have run it as partners. It was very tough on you, suddenly to have all you'd ever wanted, then to lose it. Believe me, Henrietta, if I've seemed impatient of your devotion to Godfrey's memory, it's not that I've not understood how you must have felt—only that I don't like to think you're missing out on life because of it.'

It was nicely said. Henrietta patted her necklace fleetingly. 'Thank you, Johnny. But it does make me a little cross sometimes when people seem to think if you haven't got a husband your life is empty. There's more meaning to life than just marriage, you know.'

'Of course I know it. You've lived a very useful life. But I think marriage enhances life ... or ought to. A lot more can be achieved in double harness. Oh, there's the gong. Come on down, Freckle-face. If we're to have a good long bathe we don't want to waste time.'

Waikanae was a symphony of blue and gold, with sand curving to meet the sea in a frill of white foam

43

and the sea curving to meet the sky at a lavender rim of horizon.

At the flat Henrietta had changed into a sun-frock, dazzlingly white with blue cornflowers and golden wheat splashed upon it, her brown skin glowing against it.

She kept the necklace on as they drove north, saying it was so beautiful she couldn't bear to take it off, but that Johnny could lock it in the car when they went into swim.

Her bathing-suit was coral and she didn't wear a bathing-cap but dived through every rearing breaker with complete abandon.

Johnny said, 'I'm very glad that top-knot of the other night was removable. It was glam, I know, but with your hair short, Henrietta, it's a bit more you, although——'

'Yes?' she asked, dancing in the water, '...although what?'

'Oh, never mind. I expect you're glutted with compliments.'

'Well, one more won't make me sickeningly vain. It's too frustrating to have you stop now.'

His finger flicked a wet strand of hair. 'Although I thought you looked absolutely ravishing with your hair all piled in those whirls and things. Nobody there could hold a candle to you.'

Henrietta burst out laughing. 'Of all the absurd statements! There were some top-notchers there.'

His mouth twisted. 'You never believe me when I say those things to you, Henrietta. Yet you take other things I say far too seriously. But never compliments.'

Her eyes were wary. 'I expect it's because I look on you as a brother. And one doesn't expect compliments from brothers, or look all coy abut them if they come unexpectedly.'

He grimaced again. 'I'd have thought that five years apart could have put us on a different footing. But apparently not. So to hell with the compliments and back to the brotherly horseplay!'

She tried to dodge, but too late, she was thoroughly ducked.

It probably served her right, she thought, but she was afraid of this new Johnny. He had every bit of the same power to disturb her, but an entirely new approach. It could be, of course, that he had learned a lot about women in the intervening years and knew now what they expected from men. But it didn't fool her. What she wanted from Johnny was what he'd felt for Deirdre all those years ago.

Henrietta felt memory swoop back on her ... the stabbing poignancy of seeing Johnny Carruthers look at Deirdre Seelby with his heart in his eyes. There was all the difference in the world.

That Johnny had been swept off his feet. *This* one was calculating. *This* one needed a wife. *That* one had desired a woman. And Henrietta wouldn't settle for less. It had to be all or nothing. So it looked like being nothing.

Nevertheless, there was something intoxicating ... painful yet wonderful in just being with him.

Wanganui was lying in its Sabbath quietness, in the triangle of two huge ridges and the Tasman Sea. They went up Durie Hill and up the Tower to look their fill ... back into purple ranges narrowing about the mighty river, and holding who knew what secrets in fold upon fold of height and depth and stream and ravine.

Then they drove through the town and up St. John's Hill between great trees of flowering red gum and on to the plateau-like fertile pasture-land beyond.

'I have a yen to see Mount Egmont from Kai Iwi Beach,' said Johnny. 'I get very homesick for the Alps of the South Island and just a glimpse of snow now and then reminds me that they're still down there.'

Yes, once the mountains got you, once you'd lived among them, nothing else ever quite satisfied you. You belonged.

Johnny continued: 'I was driving down from Auckland recently. I'd flown up from Christchurch but hired a car and drove back. I'd certain Ministry of Works projects to visit, mostly to see key men. I was coming home from Palmerston North and didn't dream you could—under certain circumstances—on a road quite a few miles south of there, see Egmont. It was a glorious sunset, a sort of tawny-amber one, with streaks of cloud across it, and suddenly, on the crest of a hill, I saw the perfect cone of Egmont, darkly purple, against that amber-gold light. I thought I was seeing things, because the road dipped immediately, and I couldn't credit it would be visible. But the next crest was a better place to pull in and there it was.

'It must have been some freak of distance and light and quite enchanting. I made up my mind there and then that when I got to Wellington I'd bring you up to Kai Iwi, where, on a good day, you can see Mount Egmont.'

Henrietta felt moved. This was kinship of spirit. Perhaps ... perhaps it mattered more than what Johnny had felt for Deirdre. A better foundation maybe. Didn't everyone say you needed something to build on? That when passion died down, you needed friendship and respect, the qualities that wore well. But ... but oh, how much more rewarding, how much sweeter, how much more fulfilling to have *both*.

They dipped down to Kai Iwi, where the stream widened out into a lagoon, warm and shallow, where children played happily and the water ran out lazily into the Tasman Sea. Across the lagoon ice-plant, flowering vividly, almost disguised the lookout that reminded the older people of the war years when there were enemy raiders in the Tasman and the Pacific.

Johnny said, 'I think we could have another bathe before tea, don't you?'

The water was gloriously warm, and the ebbing tide was leaving great pools behind it. Henrietta floated on her back, dreamily content with the present moment.

46

A world of salt-tanged water, sun and sea and ..
Johnny Carruthers. Last Sunday she had gone for a
sedate drive with the head of her department, his wife
and their overseas visitors, and hadn't dreamed Johnny
was in New Zealand. It seemed an aeon away.

She found he had a picnic tea in the boot of the car
and he said he'd bought the sandwiches at a quick-
lunch bar before he'd come to church.

He said reproachfully, 'I tried to trace you through
John Durant, but couldn't find him in the telephone book and the exchange didn't even have a list-
ing.'

'Oh, he's getting married next week, so he's in their
house—just—and that's all, and the phone isn't getting connected till tomorrow.'

'Don't sidetrack me. So I rang Jock McIntosh and
got his wife. She sounded so surprised I'd not known
you'd stayed the night there. I felt no end of a chump.
She said you'd been baby-sitting, wondered why you'd
not invited me round there. And you led me to believe
you were out with some chap and that I couldn't tag
along! You ought to have your mouth washed out with
soap. I hate liars. She said you'd gone home to change
for church and if I missed you I could probably catch
you coming out of service. I did miss you at the flat—I
rang—so I went hotfoot up Willis Street to St. John's.
You'll give me an inferiority complex yet, not wanting
my company.'

Henrietta, biting into a cucumber sandwich with
relish, said, 'I can't even imagine you on speaking
terms with an inferiority complex.'

She'd said it lightly enough, but his tone was serious.
'Can't you? Just shows how little even our nearest and
dearest know us. Perhaps that's inevitable. All life is in
spots, very solitary. Nobody but one's own self can
know one's own inadequacies.'

Henrietta looked swiftly down at the sand. He'd
said, 'nearest and dearest'. Oh, just a saying, not
meaning her. But one did not associate Johnny Carru-

thers, successful, seemingly an extrovert, big and bouncing, with knowing a sense of inadequacy. Then something struck her ... he'd probably never felt inadequate till Deirdre turned him down. She hadn't thought of this before, had been too taken up with her own feelings about Johnny. He must have felt very hurt that other women followed their men into remote and desolate places, but Deirdre hadn't cared enough to attempt it.

So she looked up and said gently, 'I'm sorry, Johnny. But—but you have always seemed so—self-sufficient. It *is* true that no one knows us as we know ourselves.'

He said quickly, 'But I would have thought *you* would have known.'

Her eyes met his questioningly. 'Why me, particularly?'

He frowned. 'Remember that time I found you on your own, away up the Hill of the Stars? You were eleven. I was fifteen. And you were howling your head off because there had been no letter from your mother with the mail that day. Just a little, lost, lonely kid. And I sat down beside you and told you what most boys wouldn't have liked to confess ... that I had howled myself to sleep every night for a fortnight when I'd first gone to boarding-school, and how I had dreaded holiday times till Godfrey took me to Pukewhetu. Does that add up to adequacy? Does it?'

Henrietta reached out a hand to him in a quick, warm gesture. 'No, it doesn't. I'm sorry, Johnny. Because knowing you felt like that too about your parents being overseas took a lot of the sting out of my own loneliness. It was never quite so bad again.'

He relinquished her hand and took a piece of custard pie. How prosaic! 'It helped me, too. Whenever I felt bad about not having a home to go to, I thought to myself: "Henrietta's in the same box," and I'd look forward to the vacations the more because of that. It took the sting out of Godfrey greeting his parents, when you travelled up with us. And you were a great

48

little scout. We expected you to be just as tough as we were—no chivalry. And somehow you always managed to keep up.'

Henrietta giggled. 'I was so terrified I'd be left out of any of the expeditions.'

Johnny was silent for a time, letting sand trickle through his fingers as he scooped out a hole. Then he said, 'So why be so off-putting now, Henrietta? Was it just strangeness? A reluctance to admit me back into your life on the old, selfish terms? Was I a bit demanding, expecting you to crowd out other engagements to be with me?'

She didn't answer for a moment but clasped her arms about her knees and looked out past the lagoon to the open sea.

He said sharply, 'Answer me, Henrietta, and look at me when you do.'

Reluctantly she turned to him. She said slowly, 'I'll have to be honest, Johnny. It's because of——'

Odd that so fair a man could scowl so darkly. His face looked like a thundercloud immediately. 'You mean it's because of—someone else. Right. Tell me? Tell me who? I can take it. Fair enough ... I've been away a long time. But I was mad clean through when you only cabled me, and thought you needed time.'

She said indignantly, 'You do jump to conclusions. You always did. There's no one else. Oh, there are plenty to squire me to all the functions we can't escape in our line of work, but no one special. I told you I was satisfied with life. My single life. And it will be even better back at Dragonshill. I was going to say that my—well, reluctance to let you monopolize my time was purely on the grounds of—well, it was because of your letter. I thought you might misunderstand—that you might think I could—well, accept, after this longer time had passed. I'm quite willing to take up our old friendship, Johnny, for such times as we meet, but nothing more than that. And it did seem as if—that first night, you——'

'You **mean** because I kissed you—in the way I did?'

'Yes,' she said gratefully. 'It's—not fair to any man to let him think you want—want lovemaking from him. Very few men are satisfied with the sort of companionship we had when we were kids, a sort of brother–sister relationship—but that's all I have to offer, Johnny. I'll just be here another fortnight, then away in as remote a part as you can get. We could quite enjoy a few outings. But we're not on kissing terms.'

He had his knees up now, too, his hands on them, crossed, and his forehead resting on his forearms, staring down at the sand. He said, not looking up, 'That was a test, that kiss. I had to find out if there was any chance. If you'd displayed a revulsion I'd have known it was no good. I thought—till now—that the test was a satisfactory one. You *did* respond. I thought it was better than all the arguing in the world. That——'

Henrietta kept her tone level, her voice quiet. 'Johnny, I'm not a block of marble. Anyone can know a warmth momentarily. But you see, I know if ever I know anything, that it wouldn't work. But for the short time you'll be here, we could enjoy a few outings. You'll meet someone some day, Johnny, who'll meet you more than halfway. You've been in some very lonely, womanless places too long. Here and in Australia, you'll have the chance of meeting lots of girls. I imagine you'll spend quite a bit of time in the cities, as well as in the outback.'

'Thanks very much. So nice to have one's life arranged so tidily for one. Oh, well, Henrietta, if that's what you want, so be it. How exciting ... companionship, tepid and brotherly, for the week or two you're still in the North Island. Aren't you going to have your piece of custard pie?'

She ought, therefore, having cleared the ground, to have enjoyed the rest of the day more. For one thing, in temperature and beauty of surroundings it was idyllic.

The tide ebbed out so far it seemed as if it were going to slip over the curved surface of the earth and disappear, an eerie, silent ebbing. Voices of shell-gatherers and waders sounded happily on the still air. The sun westered in purple and gold and turquoise splendour, then dusk deepened the shadows, and night clouds rimmed that flaming ball as it sank down into the sea, till there was a strange nimbus of light about it that made it look more like moonlight, save for the dazzling circle you could not bear to look into. The wet sands turned deep violet and you could see every footmark on their shining surface.

'What a very odd effect,' said Johnny. 'And somehow it reminds me of Alaska. This is like another world ... a lost world. Heavens, we clean forgot to go up the top and look for Egmont. I doubt if we could see it now.' They ran up the sandy cliff path, but only the shadowy immensity of forsaken shore and cliff-top stretched north with here and there a light twinkling on. 'Well, you'll be home in two weeks, with mountains far huger than that one about you. Lucky you!'

Henrietta said, 'I'm taking my car down, of course. How are you placed, Johnny? I'm going to Picton in the Sounds instead of to Lyttelton. Motoring right down that lovely east coast to Christchurch, then, oh, then, a few short hours and home to Queenie and Uncle Mike. Would you like to come with me? They'd love to have you for Christmas.'

Johnny, loading gear into the car, said briefly, 'No, thanks. I'll be away from Wellington before you are. I've got to be on the location of the new job.'

She said lightly, 'Oh, the hush-hush one. Secret contracts or something. But you can't keep it mum for long, can you?'

'Oh, nothing like that. Only it's something I don't want to discuss. As a matter of fact I must be away by Wednesday.'

Henrietta tried to be as nonchalantly chatty on the way home as on the way up, but she felt as flat as dishwater and her heart seemed like a lump of lead. Oh, well, she'd done it herself. She had let Johnny know she liked him only as a friend and immediately something vital had gone out of the day. Tomorrow and the next day were all she might see of him for years. He'd already been down to the Lake, renewing the links of long ago. He was a free-lance consultant on a world basis, and even if Australia, where apparently his next big jobs were, was only thirteen hundred miles away, who knew how often he'd cross the Tasman?

Monday was a colossal day. All sorts of things cropped up to make the working hours a sort of hideously jammed hotchpotch, and when her chief's wife succumbed to a chesty cold, Henrietta had to substitute for her at a private function.

Although Johnny hadn't mentioned coming to her flat when he'd left her last night, she decided it was only fair to ring and tell him she wouldn't be in.

'I thought you might come round as I'd mentioned Monday night was an off night. You might accuse me of inhospitality again. But I'll be free tomorrow night.'

He sounded politely regretful but not put out. 'And I won't be here. What a pity. I'm taking off last plane Tuesday afternoon instead of first on Wednesday morning. Good job we had an outing yesterday. Give my love to Queenie and Mike and young Douglas, won't you? And tell them I'm fit and well. Oh, I'm being paged. Take care of yourself, Henrietta ... see you again some day. Cheerio.'

She stood staring at the phone rather stupidly as he clicked his receiver home. That couldn't be all! She drew in a deep breath, held it, let it go. Well, perhaps it was typical.

> *'Johnny-come-lately,*
> *Johnny-gone-soon,*
> *Inconstant as water,*
> *As far as the Moon.'*

She shook her head impatiently. What on earth did

she want to remember that stupid jingle for now?

A thought struck her. The moon wasn't as far now. Men could reach it, walk on it, bring back souvenirs! And Australia was just two hours away, jet-flying. Oh, stop it, stop it, Henrietta. Better for you when he was in some steamy jungle in South America. You don't want Johnny with his hob-nailed boots tramping all over your dreams again. And you are still as vulnerable as any lovesick teenager. You'd built up a good life without him. Let him go.

CHAPTER THREE

ONLY ten miles to go and she'd be at the Hill of the Stars, Pukewhetu. What a welcome she'd get from Queenie and Mike!

Theirs was the second homestead on the way up the side of Lake Tekapo. Only three in all that distance. Then you came to the Pawerawera, the River of Dread, that had to be crossed before you came to Dragonshill itself. Odd the fascination that Dragonshill Station exercised. These other homesteads were remote enough, by ordinary standards, but at least they all had road access.

At Dragonshill you had to cross the river, fording the countless streams that intersected its stony riverbed in an Army vehicle, especially constructed for that sort of terrain. You could be cut off for weeks by flood or snow, truly a mountain home.

But oh, what shimmering, fairy-tale splendour ... if you could spare a glance from dodging the ruts in the road, or, at times, concentrating on staying in one particular rut. Henrietta drew into the side on the crest of a slope, to look her fill of its beauty.

When you showed strangers slides of Lake Tekapo, they thought the colouring was unreal, this milky, almost iridescent turquoise, so different from the corn-flower blue of Lake Wakatipu and Lake Wanaka, further south. Across the lake classical mountains rose sheerly in places, soaring to silver-white peaks, even now, when summer suns ought to have melted a fair percentage of the snow. Oh, how lovely was Tekapo in December. But then when wasn't it lovely? Perhaps even loveliest of all in its winter-July garb.

Her eyes swept the skyline lovingly ... Mount Erebus, the Two Thumb Range, Mount Beaudonais,

Mount Schmidt, named for Charles Beaudonais-Smith's German father, Thunderclap Peak, the Witches' Cauldron, Hurricane Peak. You couldn't see the Hill of the Dragon from here, you didn't see that till you got to Llewellyns, but round this next bend she would get her first glimpse of the Hill of the Stars.

Henrietta drove on. Queenie must have been at the lookout, scanning the road, because she was halfway across the lawn by the time Henrietta had crested the rise in the drive.

Queenie hadn't changed for years, except for the little disciplined lines at the corner of her mouth that had come when Godfrey had died and she had told herself it was a duty not to grieve outwardly too much. She had a round, eager face, with merry brown eyes, and an indefinable air of comfort. She made you think of Browning's: 'God's in His heaven, all's right with the world.'

'Henrietta, what fun to have you home! And in the district for good, what's more. Heavens, girl, you must have brought half Wellington with you! Let's leave that to Mike and Doug, and come on up to the house with you. I've just taken scones off the girdle. I ran up to the lookout as soon as I finished them. I'll just bang the gong to bring the men in. They aren't far away. They arranged the work so they'd be near the house.'

Henrietta loved that gong. Johnny had vowed years ago that it wakened every echo in the mountains and set all the horns of Elfland a-blowing. She stood there, enchanted, Queenie watching her, till every last one stopped echoing.

The men came clattering down the yard in their boots, warm in their welcome, folding her in painful hugs. Doug said, 'As soon as you've had a cup of tea, Harry, I want you to come over and see the site of our new house. Marianne and I are going to get cracking soon on constructing our garden. The men start on the foundations early in the New Year. We're getting married in March.'

Henrietta was glad for them all, especially for Mike who had every possibility of a grandson, now, to bear his name and to carry on the homestead two generations hence. And Queenie would have grandchildren to knit for, to make toys for, to fashion her gingerbread men and pikelet men for another batch of children.

The afternoon sped away. Henrietta managed to speak lightly of Johnny turning up in Wellington, said, 'He told me he'd persuaded you all not to mention he'd been here first—wanted to surprise me, as if I were still about ten and liked things to pop out of hats. But he was off again ten days ago. Here today and gone tomorrow, that's Johnny Carruthers!'

She saw Douglas catch his mother's eye, grin a little, saw Queenie just as hastily disengage her glance? Why?—Uh-huh. She thought she knew. They'd been hoping romantically. That would be it for sure.

She said, 'I always think of this place as unchanging and unchangeable, but I noticed some things. That little triangular paddock of firs, for instance. The firs were so tiny they still had netting round them to protect them from stock when I first went up to Wellington, and now they're shoulder-high. And the larches on the brow of Hundred Ridge Hill have grown so much they hide the cave on the opposite face.'

'And bigger changes still are on the way,' said Douglas, and he said it almost exultantly.

Henrietta sensed rather than saw Uncle Mike frown at him. She felt a little uneasy. She didn't want too many changes here. Something had to endure in an uncertain world.

Queenie came in hastily, 'Doug can think of nothing but wedding at the moment, though that's the way it should be. I do like to see the man excited as well as the bride. He's never to take Marianne for granted. I've dinned that into him. It's not an easy life, this, and he's got to make it worth while for her—not only at first, but always, so that she never yearns for the city lights. She's a grand girl, Marianne.'

Doug grinned, 'I've got a great example, Gwillym Richards.'

Henrietta said swiftly, 'How is Verona? I heard she's really devoted to the high country now.'

'She's the picture of felicity,' said Queenie. 'Heavens, when I remember how she fought against ever being married to a mountain farmer! She never even turned a hair when her twins were born up there, without benefit of doctor. Although she said it happened too quickly to alarm her. She had about five minutes' warning. Long enough to tell Gwillym she was ashamed of him ... a shepherd all his life and afraid to help deliver a baby. But when a second one arrived, he nearly went to pieces. He talked afterwards of moving to a place near Fairlie. Verona told him not to be daft, that she'd not have had time to get to a nursing home had she lived next door to one. And Doctor Hector Middleton came up by helicopter. Not like the old times when it would have taken days. They're such beautiful boys—fair imps, though.'

Uncle Mike looked up from stirring his tea. 'They want you over at Dragonshill tomorrow, Henrietta. Penny's dying to see you and so are the kids. You'd better stay a night or two, you're looking very tired. Too much packing and farewelling, I suppose. The road's not bad, though Doug will drive you if you'd rather. But if you go yourself, we'll ring from here to say you're on your way, then you can ring from the bank for them to come and get you. Hilary and Penny want you to stay—you'll have to fight it out over there. Nice to be so popular. But I guess Madame will have the casting vote, which means you'll be at the homestead rather than at Two Thumbs.'

Oh, it was good to be home again! What a funny word home was, what mixed meanings it covered. In Henrietta's very young days, no doubt home had been where Mother and Father were, but later when Father's diplomatic posts had been in such hazardous spots, her mother had decided, in an agony of split loyalties, that she would not take her to places in Asia where rebellions and coups were almost commonplace. Some of the time she'd been with Grandma Gunn, then Gran had died and it had been boarding-school and infrequent, painful reunitings with Mother, so briefly, when they'd take a seaside cottage somewhere and pretend it was for ever. Poor Mother, torn between the two of them. It must have been hell.

Then, in Timaru, Mother had met her school friend from Auckland days, now married and loving every moment of her life at Pukewhetu. And Queenie had found in Henrietta a substitute for the daughter she'd never had. So this had become home, the only stable, permanent thing, in Henrietta's life. Knowing it would always be there, that nothing would ever take Queenie and Uncle Mike from their home above the lake. Uncle Mike's grandfather had first taken up land there, and Douglas and Douglas's sons would farm it after him.

It wasn't a guest-room Henrietta occupied, it was always called 'Henrietta's room'. Here were cupboards where her dolls still occupied a shelf, her set of Anne of Green Gables books, A. A. Milne's and Beatrix Potter's. Her shells, her gem-stones from the riverbeds and lake-beaches of the high country, one wall covered with pictures of New Zealand birds.

Godfrey's room was still the same too and—something that gave Henrietta even more of a pang—the other bed Johnny had always occupied, and above it, his shelf of books and stamp albums. Fishing flies, faded now, tacked up, and his school photos and prizes. He too had kept a corner here, a place where one could leave the things one could not travel round the world with but were too dear to give away. Things that ought to become his sons' treasures.

Queenie was full of plans for Doug's wedding. What a mother-in-law she would make! She said, twinkling, 'They're having a separate entrance to their house from the road, I thought that would make Marianne feel more independent. Oh, there'll be a track from here for convenience sake, but that way she'll not be feeling her guests always have to arrive under the eye of her mother-in-law. It's not always ideal to live on the same property—but their gate will be two miles from ours. And the house is far enough for them to do their fighting and making-up without other people embarrassing them.'

'Cut it out, Mum. You make me feel it's inevitable we should fight.'

'It is,' said Queenie calmly, 'because neither of you are just vegetables. I hope you won't fight often, and I don't think you will, just enough to add a bit of spice to life. Henrietta, remind me to give you some rhubarb to take to Dragonshill. Theirs never does as well as ours.'

Henrietta felt she'd slip very easily into the old life here. She might never leave it again. There would always be a need for a governess in this area, and it would satisfy her so much to be with children, even if never with her own.

Hilary and Francis Beaudonais-Smith had four children, Judy, Pierre, Brigid and Noel. Though they were growing up, Noel must be eleven. But Penny and Charles' children were younger. Gregory would just start school in February and Charlotte was two. It was possible that at times when access was available to Dragonshill from the Richards' station, Four Peaks, that Verona and Gwillym and Morwyn and Ruihi would bring their children over. The Richards brothers had a private plane. Yes, it could be a way of life for Henrietta.

The next morning was a sparkling one, with a blinding light striking back from the peaks. There was some magic in driving right on into the heart of the mountains knowing that when you came to the Dragonshill garages on the banks of the Pawerawera, the road ended, and that once you were through the river, there only mountains, river-flats, valleys and basins, then, due west, the spiny back of mountain rims that marked the boundary between Canterbury and the West Coast. It also marked the boundary of the station property.

She could see the end of the lake now, where the Aranui and the Pawerawera drained into the head of the lake. A small island floated like a jewel on the bosom of the lake, the island where Henrietta and Johnny had once spent two days and a night marooned, when they'd let their boat drift away.

She ran her car into one of the lean-to garages, went into another and picked up the homestead phone connection.

Penny answered. 'Oh, how lovely, Henrietta. We're dying to see you. We've got all sorts of alterations and improvements going on. We're enlarging the schoolroom. We thought you might not be able to tear yourself away till afternoon. I'll send one of the men across to get you now.'

Henrietta hoped it might be someone she knew, Arene—who was often known by the anglicized form of his name, Alan—or Walter. It was a terrific distance, not as the crow flies, but with the track defined with poles at the worst places, winding through the shingly bed, picking its way carefully, avoiding quicksands, soft patches, choosing the firmest fords, not always going across the many streams at their narrowest points, but taking the shallowest, safest runs.

You couldn't, quite, see the homestead, but you could see the tops of the trees that sheltered round the buildings, Corsican pine, Douglas fir, and larch. Every year they had a tree-planting programme. How bleak it must have been a hundred years ago, when the first pioneers took up land here. How had they dared?

Henrietta saw dust rising from the hairpin bends of the track at the far side and went right to the edge of the high bank and looked down. Presently she'd wander down to the cutting. Then she stared in amazement.

What in the world could they want this heavy building material at Dragonshill for? There were huge concrete posts, iron reinforcing, enormous pipes. She'd seen some heavy stuff carted over the river in her time, but never anything like this. It would take much heavier transport than was available at the homestead to get it across. This stuff was on a colossal scale. What—but the truck was negotiating the last stream. She'd better get going. It would save time if she took her gear to the edge of the cutting where he could turn.

She waved and was answered by a gay salute on the horn. Henrietta picked up the mail sack she'd been asked to bring, slung the strap over her shoulder, took her small case and the bundle of rhubarb and went across. Just as she stopped the rhubarb slipped.

She slung the mail sack to the ground, bent to pick both up together, rose again and was confronted by ... Johnny!

'Surprise, surprise!' he said, grinning.

'For goodness' sake,' she said, recovering, 'and you said you hated liars. That I ought to have my mouth washed out with soap! You said you were off on your bridge project!'

He pulled a face. 'Oh, the sharp tongue of her ... and Johnny Carruthers a man who can't be dissembling however hard he tries. Henrietta, my darling, it was nothing but the naked truth I was after telling you.' He turned to the riverbed and despite the bantering tone, a ring of real pride came into his voice.

'There it is ... the site of my bridge-to-be ... the bridge over the River of Dread, Madame's dream come true! The formalities went through and were signed on her hundredth birthday. The Minister of Works is to unveil a plaque in January. Not only Madame's dream, but mine. The peak of my career ... to give Dragonshill road access.'

He grabbed the things from her, slung them into the back of the truck, seized her by the elbows and danced her round and round, to her laughing protests.

61

'Oh, girl, I can hardly believe it myself. It's so darned remote, and leads nowhere—at least what most folk would call nowhere—but it's the most fortuitous thing. You know that land that Charles and Francis gave to the National Park? It's to be opened up as an approach to a new ski-ground. It won't spoil Dragonshill, we've seen to its protection for all time, and it's the most wonderful thing that has ever happened here.

'It's really all due to Madame. She's a giddy wonder. Managed to keep it from her grandsons and approached the Government. She went up and stayed in Christchurch to fix it up, and even flew up, unknown to them, to Wellington. She had some obscure mining shares in Australia for years—you know the big boom in minerals there—well, she's sold out for quite a packet.

'She said the one legacy worth leaving to the women of Dragonshill was freedom from fear ... fear of not being able to cross a flooded river when their time was upon them, when children were ill, or injured. She contacted me months ago. This is my second visit. The first was really rushed. I swore them to secrecy as far as you were concerned.'

'But why?' asked Henrietta. 'I mean—well, you couldn't know then it could mean anything—or much —to me. I was, to all intents and purposes, completely settled in my job in Wellington.'

Johnny waved a hand. 'We'll skip my reasons. There are some things not good for you to know. Well, the whole thing hung in the balance for a while, but Madame's money tipped the scales and we're off to a good start. Fortunately, for access to this ski-field, there has to be a small bridge over Four Peaks Ravine too, so that will link up the Richards' place. In a year or two, Heronscrag will be linked too. You know Matthew Greenwood got married in October, don't you?'

She nodded. 'Yes, everyone up here was so thrilled they all wrote me about it. They say she just revels in the life up here. Imagine, when she'd been secretary to a London T.V. star.'

'Oh, well, she was Henry Dean's niece—great-niece. Guess it was born in her. She's a great lass. You'll like her.'

It gave Henrietta a strange feeling. Johnny had been away from New Zealand so long, yet seemingly she was the stranger, having everything explained to her. Yet she had come alive again. Neither the Atlantic nor the Tasman was between them. He was here ... here ... and so was she, and a job like a bridge would take a long time.

Johnny said, 'Well, hop in. Madame has done a lot of waiting in her century of living. Mountain women do, yet she was so impatient for you to arrive. She was up long before her usual time, which is ten o'clock these days ... a great concession on her part to the cancelled calendar of the years. Henrietta, do you realize that Madame was born the year Charles Dickens gave his last public reading and Napoleon the Third declared war against Prussia?'

Henrietta blinked. 'Johnny, wherever do you come by these strange scraps of information? History is the breath of life to you, isn't it? Why ever didn't you take on teaching or lecturing?'

'Because from the time Godfrey brought me to this area I just wanted to build bridges. I hated bridges till then. They took my parents away from me to the far corners of the earth. Then I saw what bridges could mean to people like the Beaudonais family, to the Richards, the Greenwoods.'

They came up out of a fairly deep stream on to dry shingle again. Henrietta felt lumpy in the throat. She'd never imagined, either, in those childhood days, that Johnny Carruthers would follow his father's career of bridge-building. He'd always said, just as that smaller Henrietta had done, that when he had a family of his own, he was going to be with them, to strike roots, to go high country farming.

She said, 'It used to be so different. Life was so clear-cut when we were youngsters. I thought I knew where I was going, and where you were going. Don't you ever want to settle down, Johnny?'

She meant in one spot. He misunderstood her. 'I'll settle down all right ... when I find a girl who'll love me enough to follow me ... camp-hopping.'

Henrietta, though she did not show it, felt blazingly mad with him. Oh, the lordly Johnny! He'd expected someone to love him enough for that. Yet he'd admitted *he* had only secondhand emotions to give any girl. He hadn't said when he could find a girl he could love. Oh, no, it had to be a girl to love *him*.

They went through nine streams, low now in summer, with a heavy thaw earlier having reduced the chances of summer freshes. Then they were grinding up the far bank on what passed for a road.

'Will your bridge follow the line of the ford?' she asked.

He laughed outright. 'Oh, Henrietta darling! What do you think a bridge that length would cost? Even if we took it straight across from here to the cutting, it would cost the earth. It's not a main highway, dill! No, we take an approach from just past the garages—that's what that preliminary stuff is for; it goes north, to Llewellyns' Bluff, and across to Kea Bluff, but in the lee of it. Charles and Francis will put in an access road from there to the old homestead and to Francis's house —in fact they've got it roughly formed now—and then the Ministry of Works will be responsible for the one to the lower ski-hut. The Alpine Club are combining with various Tramping and Climbing Clubs to put up accommodation there, chalet-style.'

'They—I mean Charles and Francis—don't mind their estate being somewhat whittled down?'

'No. It's no longer significant. Top-dressing by plane, and other modern aids and factors are bringing up the quality of the grazing here. It can support far more sheep than once. They used to be able to winter only five thousand sheep, now they can winter seven thousand. In fact just the other day Charles said the estate could support three farmers now. This is a great thing, of course. In New Zealand we have so much land that should be brought up to higher production. It's a long-term programme, but the bridge will speed it up terrifically. It will be more intensive farming.'

Henrietta had spent so long in this area years ago she could appreciate all this. These back-country stations were allowed to carry only what stock they could winter. In other days early runholders had overstocked in summer and the winter losses had been ghastly. They were all merino sheep here, agile, goat-like creatures who gave little trouble at lambing-time because their lambs were small. Their wool was superb.

Henrietta said reflectively, 'You say it could support three farms now. Does that mean they'll take Arene on as a partner? Instead of being one of the married shepherds.'

'Well, he's on a bonus system now. Almost as good, but with not quite the responsibility. Not tied the same. Charles offered him the chance, but Arene says his wife has been such a brick the way she has adapted to this life that he'll take her back to the North Island some time near her own people. Charles—a good scout if ever there was one—immediately put him on to this bonus system, so that he'll have a bit of capital behind him when the time comes.'

'Oh, then he's not got anyone particular in mind?'

Johnny said, 'There's the beginning of your welcome ... hark, hark, the dogs do bark.'

The sunshine was dry and hot, like Swiss sunshine, but these mountains had a sere and tussock-tawny splendour far removed from the green lushness of Swiss pastures. The air was full of the happy sounds she had known and loved so long ... birds calling from the homestead trees, the ceaseless singing of the mountain streams on their way to join larger streams that fed into the rivers and continued on their lusty way till they were lost in the immensity of the Lake; calves bawled, hens clucked announcements that they had done their duty, sheep baaed plaintively and as they disturbed the Canada geese they rose, honking.

Then there were human sounds, children in bathing suits racing up from the pond that served them as a skating rink in winter, doors flying open and Penny Beaudonais-Smith running helter-skelter down the slope towards them, Charles and Francis and a couple of the men advancing from a woolshed ... oh, what a welcome.

Penny's brown eyes were alight. 'What do you think about THE BRIDGE?' she demanded as she kissed Henrietta.

'Wonderful,' said Henrietta, lifting her face for a swift kiss from both Charles and Francis. 'We needn't fear sudden illness and accident half so much now. What a place this was for people who needed stitching when the river was up! I remember only one accident when the river was normal and you could get to a doctor.'

Charles chuckled. 'Never the time, the place, and the accident! I've told the kids to save up all their mishaps till the bridge is through. But let's go up. Grand'mère is dying of impatience ... oh, here she comes. Progress is a little slower these days, but look at her, Henrietta, she's as erect as ever even if she does use a stick. She hardly leans on it, though, it just gives her confidence.'

Henrietta took the rest of the slope at a glad run and folded Madame Beaudonais in her young, strong arms. 'Oh, Madame, I do love you,' she said softly. 'You make my little world seem right. You always did.'

The crêpey old face flushed, the colour bright on the high cheekbones, and the piercing dark eyes under the crown of high-piled hair, white as a cloud, softened. 'Thank you, *mignonne*. I've been so fortunate. All my dear ones, kith as well as kin, still making me feel so necessary to them, so wanted. Tell me, *chérie*, how do you like my new hair-style? Hilary has been experimenting.'

Francis reached them first, 'Isn't she a vain old thing, Henrietta?' He pinched his grandmother's cheek. 'But we like her that way. But she's still a bit tough on us. Keeps us from being too casual in our dress. At the slightest excuse she makes us get into suits.'

Charles said, 'She got a great compliment the other day. In Timaru. Grand'mère was after a new hat. She tried one on, the salesgirl looked at it from every angle then said, "No, I don't think so. It's too old for you." And Grand'mère burst out laughing and said, "Well, if it's too old for a woman of a hundred, *chérie*, whom would it suit?" But it made your day, didn't it, Grand'mère?'

'It did, but in we must go. Penny has made some delicious pastries. My mouth has been watering for them for the last half-hour. How pleased I am my sense of taste is unimpaired. I met an old man of eighty many years ago, who told me he was never tired but never sleepy, and that he was never hungry. Oh, how dreary it sounded to me! The pleasures of the table are very real ones, even if I have no patience with gluttony. Children!' as the first of them reached the group and flung dripping arms round Henrietta. 'You are wet! *Mon âme*, how you are wet. You will drench her. You have!'

Henrietta did not care. These were children she had loved from their babyhood, who were going to be her charges, a substitute for the family she would probably never have. What matter? Through them she would know the lesser dearness of achievement, bringing them educationally to a standard sufficient to enable them to embark on chosen careers.

Grand'mère led the way, 'Charlotte would not come out with me. She has turned a little shy. It will not last, you understand, Henrietta, but she, of all the children, cannot remember you and it will take a little time.'

'I won't rush her,' promised Henrietta. 'I never believe in breaking down a child's reserve. Please don't let anyone make her come and say hullo. She can observe me first a little while, then make her own approaches.'

Francis said, 'Hilary will come over later for lunch. She's finishing off some frocks for Brigid and Judy. They're going in to a Christmas party in Fairlie tomorrow, and like all women, decided they hadn't a thing to wear.'

It was all so dear and familiar, the long concrete-floored porch where, in winter, the men returning from shepherding, could stamp snow off their boots; the schoolroom that opened off it, now being considerably enlarged; the huge storeroom that looked like a grocer's warehouse, the working kitchen with its numerous gadgets and electric range, then the room that was the heart of the house at Dragonshill, the long kitchen with the diesel-operated range that never went out, long windows looking to the mountains and lake, and its picture of Mount Cook above the mantel, signed by the conqueror of Everest, Sir Edmund Hillary, who had done a great deal of climbing around here.

There was a huge table against the window, with a form behind it that could accommodate any number of Beaudonais-Smith children, plus shepherds, and it was spread with a vast array, pikelets fresh from the girdle, with a stack of yellow butter beside the plates, the French pastries Madame so loved and which Penny always made for her, a crock of cream, a bowl of fresh raspberry jam, and a pile of oatcakes, crisp and crumbly. They all fell to. Henrietta said, 'You'll have to get me out on the hill, Charles, helping with the muster, if I'm not to put on weight.'

Johnny said, 'You could do with adding a few pounds, my girl, you're far too thin. I don't like you skinny. We'll soon round you out a bit.'

Grand'mère said slowly, 'This is as it ought to have been a long time ago, yes? Johnny and Henrietta here

68

and together.' A silence, an embarrassed silence, fell upon everyone. As a rule Grand'mère was so tactful, was very annoyed with people who constantly dropped clangers—or, as she would have said, made *faux pas*.

Johnny broke it. 'Good for you, Madame. It is exactly what I've telling the silly wench myself, but this diplomatic post of hers has made her very stiff and starchy. She's got to learn to let herself go all over again.'

They expected a rebuke from Madame for this, but she merely said, 'Yes, I think so. But it will not last at Dragonshill. It never does. Look at the way Penny tried to resist my Carl. But it didn't, couldn't last up here.'

There was another silence, broken fairly quickly, fortunately, by Gregory tipping over his glass of milk. Henrietta had a flush on her cheeks and Johnny's eyes were dancing. Henrietta would have liked to have smacked him, hard. But no one would ever set Madame back, so no disclaimers were made.

Henrietta said to Penny later as they washed the dishes, 'I hope to goodness Madame hasn't got the wrong idea about Johnny and me.'

Penny said innocently, too innocently, 'What wrong idea could that be, Henrietta?'

Henrietta sighed. 'You know darned well. The trouble is that up here you're all paired off and idyllically happy. And while in Wellington they might call me the Merry Widow, surrounded by personable and eligible males and never lacking a partner for all the functions, here everyone wants to console me and as John is the only bachelor within coo-ee old enough enough for me, I can detect a matchmaking glint in every eye. It makes me furious.'

Penny giggled, 'I can see that!'

Henrietta added, 'And if anyone dares to say, "Methinks the lady doth protest too much," I shall scream. How else can you disabuse romantically-minded friends that my feeling for Johnny is purely platonic?'

Johnny's voice behind her said coolly, 'You *do* protest too much, milady.'

Henrietta swung round. 'You here! I thought you'd gone out with the others. Serves you right for sneaking up on us. I've a good mind to throw this plate at you!'

'You haven't the nerve,' he jeered. 'Not this Henrietta ... you would have once!'

The plate sailed through the air.

Johnny took a flying leap backwards, not an easy thing to do, fielded it off and, to his immense relief, caught it.

He was actually shocked. 'Henrietta, you'll be most unpopular with Penny if you throw her china round like this!'

She shrugged. Penny doubled up with laughter.

Henrietta said, 'And you called *me* a dill this morning! It's only a super-heavy plastic, idiot!'

Johnny scowled. 'Well, I didn't know they made them with posies on.' He put it down on the bench. 'I'm sure I don't know why I bother with you. We're going off in the Land Rover to Kea Bluff—the bridge approach from this side. Charles and Francis are dying to show it to you. Coming or not?'

'Coming,' said Henrietta. 'I guess they're like kids with a new toy. But I won't let them keep me too long, Penny. I expect there's a frightful lot to do, with Christmas treading on our heels, and the bridge function in January.'

Penny laughed. 'We'll pitch in tomorrow. Today you can be off the chain to visit all your old haunts. It's what I'd like to do if I were you.'

Grand'mère arrived. 'I shall come also,' she announced. 'At every possible chance I go to gaze from the Bluff across to the road on the far side, and I see a huge span joining up with the road to Tekapo. I remember how François used to vow there would be a bridge there some day. He always said it would not be in our lifetime but that our great-grandchildren would be able to go to town without wetting their feet. Of course he never even knew the comfort of the four-wheel drive truck. François never forded that river except by horse and dray, though in later years at least he had a car at the far side, to drive in to Tekapo. Never would he dream I would live to this age. I am quite determined to see it finished. I want to be able to tell him.'

'You will, Grand'mère,' said Penny, eyes a little too bright. 'I've set my heart on you cutting the ribbon and being the first to walk across it. Not this summer, but next spring.'

Madame said, 'I'll just get a chiffon scarf to tie over my hair. I do not want to spoil Hilary's hair-set!'

The three of them watched her go, three pairs of eyes smiling.

Johnny said slowly, 'It's as simple as that to Madame —a going home to François. I reckon she'll make it till the bridge is completed, but it was a good idea to have a tablet unveiled in January, just in case.... I hope you realize what interest this is going to cause, Penny. It won't be just a case of the invited guests. There'll be photographers and journalists galore and all the Mackenzie Country folk.'

Penny nodded. 'I know. So does Grand'mère. She told me that whatever happened to her afterwards, I was not to think the excitement was too much for her. She said it was going to put a seal on a century of living and suppose it was the last sunrise she ever saw, it would all be worth while, just to know the bridge project was started. She's so thoughtful. She couldn't bear us to suffer even one pang of regret. I know all the Mackenzie will be here, Johnny. But don't worry, every woman in the district is baking for it.'

Grand'mère reappeared, a filmy scarf of turquoise as blue as the lake waters tied over her high-piled hair. Johnny took her arm.

Charles drove, Madame next him, and Johnny tossed Henrietta up into the tray of the Rover before she had time to protest and clambered up after her, so Francis grinned, said, 'I'm no gooseberry,' and got in beside his grandmother. Before Henrietta could scowl, three dogs leapt up too, landing heavily on top of Henrietta and Johnny.

This track skirted the back of the homestead, threaded through a larch plantation in full leaf, and round the back of the Bluff. Even Henrietta, who knew nothing about engineering, felt this was the logical point for an approach to a bridge. A lot of work had been done on it already. The truck bounced over rough shingle, certainly, but it was already a road, and borrowed earth-moving machinery stood about.

'We've done this much ourselves,' said Charles, 'under instruction from Johnny, when he was over here before. He wanted to surprise you with this project, Henrietta, so warned the girls to say nothing to you in their letters. But tomorrow the expert gang moves in. They're going to occupy the shearers' quarters and we've an empty cottage too, and they'll bring a few huts.'

Slowly, because of Madame, they came up the slight rise. As they turned the bend to glimpse the river below, blue with the peacock-blueness of snow-fed waters, Henrietta's eyes dazzled for a moment. She had a fleeting vision of it spanned by a bridge, the sort of mind's eye mirage all engineers must know, faced by the seeming impossible tasks before them. Else they would never have the courage to begin.

She and Johnny were a little behind the other three. His eyes had been on her face, saw her expression.

His fingers fastened round hers on the hand that hung at her side. 'You saw it, didn't you? As it will be this time next year.'

'I did.' Her face lifted towards his, all enmity gone for the moment. 'I can understand now why men build bridges, even if it does take them to the opposite ends of the earth. Perhaps I part hardly with my ancient grudges. I hated bridge-building once because—like my father's job—it took yours away from you.'

Johnny said quietly, 'But your father builds bridges too ... reaches out across the gulfs of human misunderstanding ... even rebuilds bridges of friendship, blown up by war. Diplomats do. His work in establishing trade relations alone has bridged many a gulf.'

'Thank you, Johnny. Perhaps I've kicked against the pricks too long.'

'Then you've lost your resentment against your father's career?'

'Yes. He had those gifts of negotiation and diplomacy and peace-making that couldn't have been used, staying here. When I was in London for that little while, Dad and I went out a lot together. I think Mother purposely made excuses to do other things, because she felt Dad had seen even less of me than she had. And he enjoyed having me so much—even to the point of monopolizing me, that I began to realize it had cost him dearly too, as well as Mother. You know how it is with children ... because Mother came home to New Zealand to see me more often than Dad did, I thought she loved me the more.'

'So that you're beginning to understand that a man might feel he *had* to build bridges?'

'Yes. So this is why you took it as your career, after all? You began to understand your father?'

'I didn't mean that. But it can do.'

She felt at a loss, as if she had let him down somehow. As if he'd looked for a deeper understanding. His face had tightened. How lonely we all are, fundamentally, she thought. How difficult sometimes, to reach each other.

They had fallen back a little. She said slowly, 'Oh, I see. Or I think I do. And I'm sorry. Johnny, not all women are fitted to follow their men into the wilds. And perhaps they are wise. Some women have ruined their husbands' careers by just that. Others—and people often misjudge these ones, are wise enough to realize that it wouldn't work. If you happen to be the type to need security, to strike roots, then it's kinder,

73

after all, to say no.'

Oh, what was the use of trying? She saw Johnny's eyes shutter his feelings. She recognized the signs from long ago. His mouth was a thin line. She'd touched a sore spot. It must still have the power to sting, the fact that Deirdre wouldn't follow him into his wildernesses. Because they had been just that, frightening, desolate, eerie places. Dragonshill might seem remote, but it was nothing to the conditions Johnny had lived in, in the savage, beautiful deserts and jungles of the world. Where one faced not only the perils of snow and flood, but malaria, snakebite, predatory animals, hostile tribes....

Nevertheless, despite her pity, she felt a slight impatience with him. Couldn't he, even now, realize it wouldn't have done? Deirdre was purely a city type. Not to be despised for that, of course, and it had been extremely sensible of her, really, even kinder, to admit this and give him up.

She'd married six months later, someone who was now an executive with a big rubber firm. Hilary sometimes visited her, and said her life suited Deirdre perfectly. She had a dream of a home in Bryndwyr in Christchurch, entertained royally, dressed exquisitely, often travelled with her husband to the large and exciting cities of the world and revelled in every moment. A sort of perennial butterfly, but beautiful, oh, how beautiful. So flawlessly lovely you almost tired of the perfection. At least women did. Not men. And apparently Johnny still——

Henrietta returned to the present and satisfied Madame with her delight and appreciation of the project. She said, gazing across the river, 'I never dreamed that from here it was so short a distance.'

Madame nodded. 'This was the gap François always said ought to be bridged some day. I'm so glad Johnny found it the logical place. It makes it right for me, a fulfilment, almost as if François himself had planted the vision in Johnny's heart.'

How odd to suddenly envy a woman one hundred years old! Madame had known losses beyond bearing at times ... her babies who had never drawn breath because there had been no one to save them, and the only child who had survived, the mother of Charles and Francis, had died some years ago, and her husband, Carl Schmidt, before her, yet at least Madame had *lived*. She had known wifehood and childbirth and had seen her grandchildren and great-grandchildren grow up about her.

Henrietta King looked down at her left hand and twisted her wedding ring round her finger. And what was she? A widow who had never been a wife. Who would love other people's children, her pupils, very dearly, but would never know a downy head against her breast. And why? Because Johnny Carruthers only wanted her as his wife because he thought *she* had what it took to follow him around the world. He had an affection for her, yes, but not the kind Henrietta wanted, craved. Perhaps she was a fool. No doubt compromises had to be made, you had to take what you could get, maybe, but ... oh, it was no good. It had to be all or nothing. Unless Johnny loved her as she loved him, they would go their ways apart.

CHAPTER FOUR

MOST folk thought of life in these remote ranges as having an idyllic, dreamy quality, far removed from the madding crowd and the rat-race of city life, but would have been surprised at the pace they maintained.

Even with all this modern convenience, with the greatest blessing of all, the power link-up, the sheepstation had to be, in the main, self-supporting. Apart from the household work, the correspondence lessons, there were many jobs done on the station that in a less remote area would have been done by other tradesmen. The men could turn their hands to almost anything and many things were forged in the blacksmith's shop to save a trip to Tekapo, besides the shoeing that was done.

At this time of year, too, the men were away from the homestead a lot, up the valleys, because lambing was so late here at Dragonshill, starting in November, so they were still tailing, setting up portable yards wherever necessary.

They were good all-rounders, these men, and Henrietta found Johnny wasn't tied to his bridge work, but was away out on the truck, or the horses, up the riverbeds with the others.

She remarked on this to Charles one night when Penny had asked her to fetch some writing paper from Charles's office and she'd found him there.

Charles looked up from under his sandy brows, his glance keen.

'But surely you, of all people, would realize Johnny's true love is for the land, for sheep?'

Henrietta scowled. 'Why me, of all people?' she demanded.

There was a directness about Charles that was extremely satisfying, if at times disconcerting. He said simply, 'Because you are closest to him.'

Henrietta didn't reply right away. Then she said slowly, 'You mean because the rest of you up here belonged, and Johnny and I were the visitors, so we paired off? And people still naturally pair us off?'

Charles considered that. Finally he said, 'No, I don't think I had that in mind at all. It's more fundamental than that. Simply that you're two of a kind. I can't analyse it, Henrietta. It's just a fact, something you know instinctively.'

She stood in front of his desk, gazing over his shoulder through the open door that led into the tiny glassed-in porch beyond it that had windows looking eastward. The Hill of the Dragon reared its queer shape beyond the homestead trees and someone had pinned a star on the tip of his nose. Beyond it were the peaks of the Two Thumb Range.

Then she brought her gaze back to Charles, waiting. She said, 'Other people seem to know it instinctively, Charles, but not me. Anyway, this is beside the point. If Johnny's real love was the land why did he go off to build bridges? Why? He didn't even stay in New Zealand to give this country the benefit of his training.'

Charles said slowly, 'I think you could work out the answer yourself. When he first took on engineering it wasn't just a wish to join his father. He wanted to serve New Zealand, and most of all the high country runs that some day might be able to build bridges. He'd have stayed here but for one thing. It's always happening.

'The woman a man wants is out of reach, so he tries new places in an endeavour to forget. But there comes a time, if he's put his roots down deeply enough, when he comes back. And sometimes there's a second chance.' He looked at her sharply. Why? Not a second chance with Deirdre. Oh, he meant herself. Charles continued, 'Now is that time for Johnny. If he leaves

77

again he may never come back. Whether or not he stays depends.'

Henrietta didn't ask, 'Depends on what?' She knew, and Charles knew, and he knew she knew. So she said crisply, 'Penny wants some of that headed paper out of the second right-hand drawer of your desk, please?'

Charles gave it to her and she went away. He sat at his desk smiling to himself, shook his head, and went on with his stock-book.

Henrietta went through to her room and gazed out of her window. Odd, wasn't it? They all saw it Johnny's way. They thought she ought to try to keep him here. They did not even gloss over the fact that he'd broken his heart over Deirdre. As if it were her—Henrietta's—duty to make up to him for this! Nobody guessed what it would do to her to be a substitute, a second-best. Perhaps she had been too clever at concealing her feelings. They thought her a sensible, controlled sort of person. They wanted a wife for Johnny more than a husband for Henrietta. It was hardly fair.

Yet they were all such dear, dear people and she had an idea Charles was wrong about John Carruthers. She doubted if he would ever settle anywhere. He wasn't the homesick schoolboy he had been once, loving the land, and its symbolic stability. He needed the challenge of the great chasms and gorges of the earth's crust, pitting his brain against seeming impossibilities, thrusting roads through swamps and mountains and forests by bridging what had been for centuries unbridgeable.

Johnny had never been able to withstand a challenge, a dare. That was why he was so cussed and determined now, to make her his wife. Simply because she was resisting him! And after Deirdre, she was the next-best-thing. Ah, pah!

Penny would be wondering where she'd gone and needing the paper. But when she got back Johnny was there. He must have eaten across at the hut with Walter and the other shepherds. He was freshly shaved and showered and he had on long tussore-coloured trousers, part of his tropical kit, and a nylon shirt in cream. He'd slipped on a brown, cream-spotted cravat in deference to Grand'mère's liking for civilized garb for the evenings in her sitting-room.

Henrietta, unnoticed, paused in the doorway. This was what she was, so often, a looker-on at life. Madame, her white hair resting against the faded rose brocade of her winged chair, her feet on a beaded footstool, looked as if she had stepped out of a frame on the wall. Penny was curled up on a fluffy white lambskin rug, small and brown and contented, both women listening as Johnny read aloud from one of Madame's scrapbooks, priceless possessions compiled for eighty years.

Grandpère Beaudonais had, even in their hardest times, seen to it that she had been kept well supplied with magazines and books and she had garnered every snippet, every poem she had liked, to be read over and over again in those times when Dragonshill had been cut off from the rest of the world by the rising river or by deep, silent, frustrating snow.

Penny had once said that when Madame was gone from them, her heart would be with them still, in these scrapbooks.

Johnny was saying, 'I like this ... listen. Charles Lamb said it: "There is more reason for saying grace before a new book than before a dinner." And this too, by Wordsworth:

' "Dreams, books, are each a world; and books, we know,
Are a substantial world, both pure and good;
Round these, with tendrils strong as flesh and blood,
Our pastime and our happiness will grow." '

Penny chuckled suddenly and got up. 'There's a bit, near there that Grand'mère cut out of the *Australian Woman's Mirror* in the thirties ... in their Said About Men column. I've proved it over and over. Let me see, Johnny. Oh, yes, here it is: "No man can, or will, use a safety-pin in an emergency. And suppose he has a dozen shirts with every button intact, some devilish instinct will lead him to the very one with a button missing." '

Johnny chuckled too. 'Don't be so mean, Penny. I'm reading nice, peaceful, uncontroversial things. Madame is in the mood for poetry, she says. Anything in particular, Madame?'

Madame turned her head towards him. 'Yes, something I thought of today. It's on page fifty-eight of that scrapbook, Johnny. I ought to know. It was my greatest comfort when François died. He had clipped it out of a newspaper for me years before, saying it would comfort him if I died first. And now—can you see it, *mon fils*?'

'Yes, this will be it.' Johnny read it aloud. Henrietta still waited in the shadows of the hall, unobserved, but observing. How sweet it was, to gaze her fill upon Johnny's features, his ruggedness, his dearness, unnoticed.

> *"But 'tis an old belief*
> *That on some solemn shore,*
> *Beyond the sphere of grief,*
> *Dear friends shall meet once more.*
>
> *Beyond the sphere of time,*
> *And Sin and Fate's control,*
> *Serene in endless prime*
> *Of body and of soul.*
>
> *That creed I fain would keep,*
> *That hope I'll not forgo,*
> *Eternal be the sleep,*
> *Unless to waken so."* '

Johnny waited a moment, not to break the spell of the words, then said, 'It was by John Gibson Lockhart, who was born in 1794. Let me see ... that was the year

Edward Gibbon the historian died, Madame, and we —at least the English—were at war with France.'

Madame said, 'Oh, thank you, Johnny. I so like to fix dates in my mind. Lockhart. He died before I was born. How wonderful to have something one said live on for the comfort of generations yet unborn.'

In the light of the oval red reading-lamp by Johnny's side, Henrietta saw him look across at Madame with affection in his eyes. He said, 'Just as the things you have said, Madame, will live on. All my life I will remember the things you told me when I was a boy, and all you've gathered together in these pages will delight our children's children in the years to come.'

He twinkled, 'But you'll leave something more concrete too—literally concrete. In your bridge. Yes, yours. Even if subsidized by the Government. I got word just today that it's to be known as the Beaudonais Bridge and the plate on it is to say:

"To keep in imperishable memory
the steadfast courage
Of François and Charlotte Beaudonais
who tamed the high country
And rescued it from barrenness into rich
and full production." '

Charlotte Beaudonais sat upright and turned to him, as eager as a schoolgirl, her almost black eyes bright with unshed tears.

'Johnny, my dear, *dear* Johnny! *You* arranged this for me, for me and François. *Ma foi*, but it makes me so happy. Oh, but how blessed I am. Blessed in this younger generation who will follow us here.'

Johnny laughed, a little embarrassed, which was unusual for him, but pleased too, at being included as one of the family, Henrietta sensed.

Madame said softly, 'I hope that some day, Johnny, someone pays a tribute to you, too, that will please your heart as much as this has pleased mine.'

Johnny's eyes dropped to the scrapbook open on his knee, then he burst out laughing. 'Looks as if someone has done it already. What do you know! Listen to this:

"Oh, who shall sing the Summer in
Now Johnny is away...."'

Even though no one knew she was there, Henrietta shrank back still further into the shadows. She could hardly bear this.

He didn't read more than the two lines aloud, but she thought he read it to himself. He must have, for presently he said, 'It was written to someone who'd gone away in World War Two. I hope her Johnny came back.'

Grand'mère said, a smile in her voice, 'You are like me, Johnny, a sentimentalist. There was an old Scots woman who lived in a little cottage in Tekapo years ago. She said once, "I've aye liked happy endings." There's many a book I've read that has saddened me because it had what they called an artistic ending. Realism. Just as if happiness isn't as true to life as unhappiness.'

Johnny said, closing the scrapbook, 'Yes, I like happy endings too. Not that they always happen out of the blue. Sometimes they have to be contrived purposely, worked for. Sometimes they have to be achieved out of what appears second-best. I've no patience with the sort of person who nurses grief. Who won't be philosophical and carry on with life after a setback, or a loss. You did, Madame.'

Madame said softly, 'But not at first, or willingly. It took me time, Johnny. I was not always proud of my—my more feeble hours.' She seemed to shake off that thought and said, 'I almost lost that poem, the one about the Johnny who went away. It disappeared from my scrapbook, about the time Gregory was born, I remember. I thought it had come unstuck and that I'd

82

find it, loose, but no. Then one day, long, long after, I was amazed. It was back, neatly stuck in again. And Penny and Hilary vowed they'd not done it. *Incroyable*. One of life's minor mysteries, that. Odd how these things tantalize one's mind, yes?'

Penny said hastily, 'Must be some quite ordinary explanation. There has to be. I've puzzled over things like that sometimes. They always turn out to be so simple. If Henrietta doesn't bring me that notepaper soon, I'll not get my letter written. I expect Charles has delayed her ... they were talking astronomy the other night. I'll guarantee he's got her out on the porch pointing out stars.'

Johnny got to his feet. 'I'll go in search of her, Penny. I know a fair bit about stars myself. I'll take over and send Charles back with the papers if she's so keen.'

Henrietta turned swiftly and silently, melting into the shadows of the unlit hall. She rattled a door-knob and came briskly into the room before Johnny could reach the door.

Henrietta said, 'Penny, you'd think I was never coming. I went into my room to shut my window and stayed there, star-struck. The moon is very high and it's striking back a pale glimmer from the end of the lake. It looks like a lost world. And the stars seem nearer than I've ever seen them—or is it just that there is no competition here from sodium lamp-standards or neon lighting?'

'Good show,' said Johnny. 'I've just told them I was coming to show you the stars. Penny thought Charles was doing it from his porch and was seething with jealousy. Come on, Henrietta, my darling.'

She shrugged. 'I've done my star-gazing for tonight. Penny has wakened my conscience. I think I'll write letters too.'

'No, you won't, my lass. It's a sheer waste. Never again might there be just that light on the lake, just those same clouds drifting across those extra-bright stars. I've been meaning to do this ever since I came home. It's completely fascinating viewing the stars from a different angle. Out you come.'

His fingers were bruisingly hard on her arm, so she went with him.

The moment they stepped outside, the magic of the Dragonshill world was all about them. The heat of the day still seemed to be imprisoned in the valleys, despite those snowy peaks. It was very rarely one could wander round outside here without a cardigan, at night.

Johnny's hand was under her elbow, warm, comfortingly close. This terrain was rough, with the garden lawns fitting round great outcrops of rock. They went down past the willows of the farm cottages on a track that gleamed as white as sunbleached bones because this stretch was of crushed quartz, turned through a gate by the creek and went along beside it, towards the end of the shimmering lake.

Instinctively they turned left and began to climb towards a huge upthrust rock they knew of old. Grand'mère had always called it the Rock of Ages. It was cleft from top to bottom, and looked south to where the rivers flowed into the lake. It had a ridge at one end that made a comfortable seat, and a sort of parapet, as if it had been lovingly fashioned by God for shelter from the storms.

But they stood a long time, faces upraised, with Johnny pointing out star after star.

Henrietta said, 'Only since I've been in Wellington have I been at all knowledgeable about the stars, and even now what I know is infinitesimal. There was a chap in the department very keen. He used to take me to the Observatory. I felt he wakened me to the awareness of a new world—though probably ninety per cent of the world's people felt that when the first man stepped out on to the moon.'

Johnny nodded. 'Yes. It brought a new dimension into our lives.'

'When did you first get interested in the stars? I can't remember you ever taking much——'

'I've been in some places these last few years since we drifted out of each other's lives where there wasn't much else *but* stars. If you're deep in a steamy jungle—and to a chap used to this sort of space it can be very frightening—claustrophobic, in fact—and there seems to be nothing but undergrowth and creepers crowding in on you and threatening to suffocate your mental processes, you are very glad to look up at the uncluttered immensity above you and know you could breathe up there. So you become familiar with the stars. It's also a safety measure. Some day you might lose your compass. Good to know you could find your way out by the stars.'

Henrietta shivered suddenly.

Johnny said, 'Good lord, not cold, are you? You couldn't be?'

She shook her head. 'Not physically. Just that the thought of you in such jungles gives me the creeps.'

She sensed the smile in his voice. 'That's better. Nobody would have known you cared where I was, all those years. Coming out of that cocoon of yours a little, aren't you? That's what Dragonshill does for you. It's not an artificial world, it's a real world, with real values.'

Henrietta said quickly, 'It's amazingly warm for here, isn't it? The nights in Switzerland were like this, warm and mild.'

He laughed, rather derisively, 'That's it ... the minute a conversation gets anywhere near the personal, steer it away ... talk about the weather. I wonder you didn't say, "Turned out nice again, hasn't it?" Really, Henrietta! I wonder if you know how you exasperate me. You're just like that girl in "The Sound of Music" —Maria. You know what they sang about her? Wasn't it like trying to hold a wave upon the sand ... like trying to hold a moonbeam in your hand. That's you. Insubstantial—as elusive as a cloud. And once I always knew where I was with you—a yes-no person. But now you can't give a straight answer to any question!'

She said a little wearily, 'It was just that I don't want to argue all the time, Johnny, to be on the defensive. And it did remind me of Switzerland. I remember a night like this under the mulberry trees round the waterfront at Brunnen on Lake Lucerne.'

His voice warmed immediately, 'Brunnen ... you were staying there? Did you love it, Henrietta? The expresses hurtling through on their way to Milan ... the Rhone Glacier with its ice-blue tunnel ... the William Tell country, and, opposite Brunnen, Switzerland's Runnymede, their Field of Ruttli?'

She nodded. 'I was in luck. I was there on the first of August, their National Day. I was at the Grand Hotel du Lac, and we sat out on the balcony and watched the fireworks on the barges at night, afloat on the lake. But the most beautiful of all was the way they freed thousands of paper lanterns, candlelit, on the bosom of the lake, floating like fireflies on the dark waters. It was a dream.'

His voice was sharp with surprise. 'I stayed at the Grand Hotel too ... must have been some time after you, though. It completely fascinated me ... did you know it had been used way back in the last century as a sort of apartment house for most of the families of the crowned heads of Europe?'

'Yes, that was why all those portraits—so familiar most of them—crowded the walls. I thought it was glorious. The owner—then—had been an artist of skill and had painted most of his royal guests.'

He nodded, his eyes on her upturned face, eager, younger, very clear in the bright moonlight.

She said, 'Oh, I'm so glad you were there. I was with a tour—Mother and Father couldn't come—so I feel all these things are locked up in me. I can't say to anyone, "Remember that darling little village of Morschach, tucked into the lap of one of the hanging valleys, or the pinewood track that zigzagged down from Seelisberg, opposite Brunnen, to the Field of Ruttli." I'll never forget the magic of the sound of the alpenhorn being played there ... it reminded me so much of you saying that the Pukewhetu gong wakened all the horns of Elfland.'

He said, 'So you did spare me a thought now and then. We ought to have seen it together. These things shared are doubly beautiful. Now, Henrietta, *don't* retreat into your shell. Be yourself, girl. Tell me, did you take a trip to Grindelwald, through Interlaken, and Brienz?'

She nodded. 'And saw the Junfrau, on a cloudless day, and that huge waterfall, spilling from the cliffs above the little town ... um ...?'

'Lauterbrunnen. We'll put on some slides here one night and show the others and just revel in all that beauty again ... the splash of red geraniums in window-boxes against the oiled brown of the wooden houses and overhanging eaves ... and everywhere the pungent smell of the manure they use so they can take several crops a year off their small pastures.'

'That's a romantic thought,' said Henrietta, wrinkling her nose and smiling.

He disregarded that. 'And did you see that incredible face of the Eiger the day you went to Grindelwald, and did you feel immensely small?'

She nodded, 'And the funicular railways, with red and blue trains, vivid against the lush green ... Oh, Johnny, do you think that sort of thing will come to our own mountains some day? That little villages will nestle against them, and garden flowers will splash vivid colour against our more remote lakes. They do at Lake Wakatipu, of course. But the others?'

His face was serious. 'It will come. It's coming gradually now. But the little villages won't appear in our lifetime, probably, but in our grandchildren's time.'

Would they ever, either of them, have descendants? Henrietta wondered. Though he was speaking in a general sense, not a personal one.

He continued, 'I feel our bridge is the first step. Oddly enough I first knew I must make it a reality, one morning at five, in the Grand Hotel. My bedroom was right over the front, almost bang in the middle. Did you happen to notice that on the first floor the bedrooms opened on to tiny balconies and you could, if you wished, step out on to a sort of verandah roof that jutted out and was covered with turf to give the illusion of being on ground level.

'You looked up the lake towards Mount Pilatus above Lucerne—though you couldn't see it—and down the passes in the direction of Milan. And all along the water and up in the hanging valleys were the villages. I thought of the wonderful holidays people had there and determined that some day, in my own land, I'd make access easier. I'm sure I felt as a poet would feel ... inspired. I just suddenly knew that when my contracts were completed, this was what I must do. Perhaps your ghost had left something of Dragonshill behind you, Henrietta.'

She said, smiling slowly at the absurdity, 'Johnny, you said almost bang in the middle. You wouldn't remember your room number?'

'I do. It was a double room because they weren't full up and I asked for that one because of the view.' He told her the number.

She looked amazed and delighted. 'That was mine. I sat out on that balcony at a small round table and watched the first steamers putting out across the lake on the morning of their National Day, long before breakfast. The daughter of a friend of Mother's was with me, but she was fast asleep in the other bed. I was glad, because you want to watch a scene like that in silence. What an extraordinary coincidence!'

'A nice one, don't you think? Some'—he hesitated and said—'Some coincidence,' rather lamely. Then, 'I got so carried away by Swiss architecture, I imagined what one of those houses would be like, here at Dragonshill, with boxes of geraniums splashing scarlet among the tussocks. Can you imagine that too?'

He had drawn a little nearer.

Henrietta said swiftly, breathlessly, 'Oh, look, that tiny cloud has disappeared from the top of Mount Beaudonais. And there are two stars very close to the peak. What are they?'

'No idea,' said Johnny. 'They're entirely unimportant, I'm sure, in the world of astronomy. Tell me, Henrietta, who was this man who wakened you to the world of stars? Unattached?'

She burst out laughing. 'He had five children, nine grandchildren and a great-grandchild expected. Certainly he had married young, but he was more than twice my age. He was very rotund and wore a watch-chain and old-fashioned suits. Not that I minded the rotundity. I like men of that age to be portly, don't you?'

Johnny chuckled. 'I do, come to think of it. Glad you like 'em that way, Henrietta, because Mother vows I'll be just like Dad before I'm fifty, and goodness knows *he's* portly.'

She turned away a little. She must *not* take him up on every point. He did it to be annoying, as if they were bound to be married by then. It was much harder to cope with than if he were definite. His proposal by letter she had promptly and curtly refused by cable. But this was insidious. He hoped she'd slip into accepting the situation.

He said, 'But there must have been plenty of unattached ones. In fact, I know there were. I saw them at that reception. *They* were keen. *You* were not. Was it always that way?'

She heaved a sigh. 'Yes.'

'None of them stir you out of your hundred years' sleep at all, Sleeping Beauty?'

'No.'

'Why not?'

'Oh, Johnny, Johnny, you *know* the reason why!'

The moment she said it she felt aghast. It had been forced out of her.

But he said, quietly, 'Godfrey's memory?'

For one tempted moment she felt like shouting the truth at him, of saying: 'No, not Godfrey's memory ... my stupid attachment to someone who doesn't really care. Not the way I want him to, anyway. *You*.'

The moment passed. Long years of self-discipline had done that much for her. Made it possible for her to save her pride, the only thing she had left.

She said instead, 'John Carruthers! Must you drag that in all the time? You said in Wellington that Godfrey was gone and to get on with life. I'm trying to do just that. I'm looking forward tremendously to my work as governess here. I'm brimming over with ideas for it. I feel—just as you do with your bridge—that by doing this I'm making some repayment to these wonderful people of the Mackenzie Country who made our childhood less sad. It irritates me tremendously, John, that people seem to think a woman's life without a man in it is a desert! There are lots of other things in life besides love and marriage. And anyway, I still have my dreams about what marriage can and should be. And I'll never, *never* settle for second-best.'

She thought her calm tone would add weight to her words, be utterly convincing. But he seized her by the upper arms, his fingers biting in.

His eyes were searching hers. God send she did not give anything away. He said intensely, 'Henrietta, it was an idyll, I know. As it *would* be, with Godfrey. Heaven knows I realize I could never measure up to him. Godfrey had that quality—I don't think I can analyse it, but you'll know, you must know, what I mean. Something that was pure spirit. I should know, none better, that sometimes one particular person has a place in one's heart no one else has. But often these things are no more than that ... an idyll, not made of good earthy stuff. I *am* earthy, and I know it, but I think it's a stuff that would endure.

'We ought not to let what was impossible—at the most only a dream—take the substance from us. We've always been such pals—except these last five years—we like the same things, laugh at the same things, even sometimes share a kindred tear—I know I can't offer you a grand passion such as—well, let that go—but I feel we could have a very satisfying life together.'

She didn't answer, because, although he did not know it, she was resisting capitulating with every inch of her being. She wanted to accept him on those terms, on any terms, but that would be madness, because she could not stand a lifetime of longing for what he could not—quite—give her.

He gave her a shake. 'Don't go in on yourself. It's maddening. You retreat into regions where I can't reach you. I've tried to understand, but naturally, being a man, I can't—quite—enter into a woman's feelings. You've been a wife. I've never been a husband. I expect you feel you've known the best, and don't want any further experience to overlay that perfection. But I can't think it's a healthy attitude. No, I can't. I won't expect—wouldn't expect—what you gave Godfrey. Are you frightened I wouldn't understand that?'

She said 'No,' through stiff lips. Then, 'It isn't that. I think you *would* be quite understanding—I——'

He broke in, a spark in his eye, 'Henrietta, good lord ... surely you don't think I'm offering you one of those daft marriages in name only? I suppose in certain circumstances they could happen, but not for me. It would be more than flesh-and-blood could stand. And we'd both want children, anyway. I meant I wouldn't expect that same, overwhelming and idealistic young love you gave to Godfrey, that's all. Now *will* you quit being a tragedy queen and come down to earth?'

But he'd gone the wrong way about it. Now was the time when she might have told him she had never been a wife, but he'd underlined once more the fact that he thought she'd felt for Godfrey what he had once felt for Deirdre. Very bluntly, in fact she'd never forget his voice saying, 'I know I can't offer you a grand passion ...' and '*I* should know, none better, that sometimes one particular person has a place in one's heart no one else has.'

She didn't want a husband who had an ideal enshrined. Oh no.

She supposed it was different for men. A man needed a wife for the everyday relationship of home-making as well as the deep, fundamental hunger of the man–woman relationship. So men could and did settle for second-best. Some women accepted this and achieved great, if not perfect, happiness. But Henrietta could not.

She said, 'Johnny, your fingers are bruising me. How will I explain those bruises away when I'm swimming with the youngsters tomorrow? I do wish you wouldn't get all intense like this. I used to enjoy our old friendly relationship. I don't mean just when we were kids, I mean when we first grew up. Can't we get it back and leave the fireworks to those who like them? Why can't we?'

His fingers had instantly relaxed their pressure, but he said, 'Why can't we? Don't you know? Because no relationship ought to be static, it ought to deepen, harmonize, merge ... like this.'

He slipped his arms about her quite gently, as if knowing that this time she would not twist away from him. He said, 'Oh, Henrietta, Henrietta darling, you funny little freckle-faced thing. You can't be as naïve as all that. What a mixture you are! In Wellington you were so sophisticated you scared all hell out of me. I thought I'd never get through to the real you. So I washed your face looking for the freckles. They were there all right, but you've still got a protective covering on you like an armadillo. And I doubt if you're deceiving anyone but yourself. Let yourself go a bit ... like this. ...'

His hand was between her shoulder-blades, exerting gentle but increasing pressure. She felt spellbound. She looked up into his face very searchingly. He began to smile, a slow smile, with lips and eyes. Then he bent his head to hers. At first he was gentle, then, as he found no resistance, even a little warmth, the pressure became harder. But it wasn't a demanding kiss. It was a kiss exchanged, not given or taken. This was a Johnny she did not know. Perhaps a Johnny worth having. He wasn't madly in love with her, no, but ... sweet. And that was an adjective she had never associated with Johnny's behaviour before, except with his whistling, those gay, sweet, tangled tunes that changed so rapidly from one to another, tantalizing melodies, never finished.

How strange to be able to stand within a man's embrace and think all this. It was almost as if one had come into safe harbourage at last. *Almost.*

He lifted his mouth and put his cheek against hers. 'See...?' he asked. 'Not the heights perhaps, but—rather enchanting, don't you think?'

She laughed suddenly, the sort of carefree laugh one hears from a child, and he said, 'That's better. I've always liked comedies better than tragedies. You used to laugh like that at Pukewhetu, feeding the ducks on the stable-pond. Sheer mirth in it. There has been too much heartbreak, too much care these last few years, I think. Let's make up our minds to shake off a few years, grow young again.'

She wouldn't quite commit herself. 'Perhaps,' she said, and with that he had to be content.

There was harmony between them as they wandered back to the house. But they kept off personal topics. They talked of other places on the Continent, sharing memories of the spots they had both visited, apart.

Many places only one knew, but they could recall many together. Heidelberg Castle with all the traffic of the Rhine passing along below, the Rhine Falls, split by a huge rock into cascades of foam; fairy-tale Luxembourg, the market-place at Trier, bright with flowers, with baskets of beans and tiny cucumbers, and a small German town they had both lost their hearts to, Villingen, with its Roman walls, its archways and cobbles.

They came to the house. Henrietta looked up at him with an appeal in her eyes. 'Keep it this way for a bit, Johnny, it's been so pleasant.'

He laughed. 'Yes, wasn't it pleasant? So let's try it again.'

He knew she hadn't meant that, but mischief danced in his eyes and Henrietta found herself letting him kiss her again, but lightly, laughingly. When they drew apart again they found that light was now streaming out from the sitting-room where Charles had switched on.

The two outside looked in at the group, and stood, enchanted. Madame's gesturing hands were flashing with the diamonds she always wore. Charles was standing, as big and blond as Johnny; Penny, with her smooth brown colouring, was still curled up on the floor. She said something at that moment that made the other two laugh, and Charles bent to her and ruffled her hair, that in his eyes which made Henrietta fiercely envious of her.

Madame's gaze rested upon them, benignly.

'Lucky Charles and Penny,' said Johnny. He sounded wistful, and when Johnny sounded wistful Henrietta knew she was wax in his fingers, so she said swiftly, 'Isn't Madame wonderful? Age has only beautified her. It must be something of the spirit, I think.'

'She's very happy that you and I are here, together.'

'I know, but——'

'No buts tonight ... you've only just stopped bawling me out every time I open my mouth. Let's just accept things as they are. I'd like this to be a happy, happy month for Madame. She won't embarrass us, Henrietta. And you must allow an old lady her dreams.'

Not embarrass them! Far worse than that! She dropped a mighty spanner in the works.

Charles had prepared a cup of tea. There were buttered scones and cream-filled sponge-drops, to which Madame did full justice. Then she said she would retire. She turned at her bedroom door, said, 'Oh, by the way, when I got up from my nap this afternoon and you were all down at the swimming-hole, I rang Christchurch and invited Deirdre down for the bridge ceremony. I don't think anyone thought about her. Perhaps my memory is not quite gone yet. She jumped at the chance. She seems very lonely. You see, Rodney has been in Singapore two months. *Bon soir*, all of you.'

Nobody spoke. Penny looked utterly dismayed, Charles scowled, and Johnny? Henrietta caught a too-revealing look for a swift instant before he schooled his features into impassiveness. But it was enough. Henrietta felt someone else could speak first.

Charles took the plunge. 'What makes her think her memory's so good?' he growled. 'She must have clean forgotten you used to be engaged to Deirdre, Johnny. Hell's bells, what the devil can we do?'

Johnny began to fill his pipe. He looked across at Charles, 'Why, what were you thinking of doing?'

Charles actually spluttered. 'Well, what I'd like to do is ring Deirdre and cancel the damned invitation, tell her it's too confounded awkward. But I suppose——'

Penny sparked up hopefully, 'Oh, could we? I——'

Johnny said, 'What's all the fuss? She's married, isn't she? It's not like a couple breaking up and friends trying to patch it up. Even divorced couples meet these days. It's happening all the time. You must know that, surely. They call it being civilized. I shouldn't care for it myself, but a broken engagement is nothing.'

Penny said hotly, 'But I can't stand her. I know everyone says there's no harm in her, but I'm not so sure. They mean she never does any intentional harm, but most of the trouble in the world stems from people like that. And I never did like her type—wanting every man in the place, attached or unattached, dancing attendance upon her.'

Charles, recovering himself now, said, cocking an eye at her, 'Sounds like little green apples to me. This is very interesting. Tell me, my love, did she ever make you suffer any pangs of jealousy? I'd love to think you could be jealous. It's the one thing missing in your nature.'

Penny was wide-eyed. 'You must be stark, staring mad! You must know what I went through when I thought you were in love with Verona!'

'Well, you hid it so darned well, I never knew. It would have tickled my ego no end. I mean, you told me what you'd thought, but I didn't dare hope you'd actually seethed with it.'

Penny got up and fired her cushion at him.

Johnny said, 'Oh, not to worry, any of you, on my account. After all, she's been married more than four years. Any family? No? Oh, well, perhaps she's not the maternal type. But she's probably a different person altogether. Henrietta, do you want a turn outside before turning in? It's still stifling.'

'No, thank you,' she replied, getting up, 'it's too late. And Judy and Brigid want me to go for an early morning ride with them. Goodnight, all.'

In her room she stared at her reflection unseeingly.

Deirdre ... here. That was all it needed. How foolish of her to know a moment or two of enchantment up on the Rock of Ages tonight. To believe, deceiving herself, that perhaps in time, Johnny could come to care for her in the way she had always dreamed he might! One look at Deirdre and he would know all over again the pain, the disillusionment and the longing.

CHAPTER FIVE

IT was significant that he did not come to ride with them next morning.

Had he been in the same mood as the night before, Henrietta knew he'd have been there with the girls, saddling up, by the time she emerged. And it wasn't as if the men had roped him in for some early morning job, for he was still in his bed. Had he had a sleepless night after Grand'mère's statement?

When Brigid, Judy and Henrietta came in, fresh from their gallop, he was just coming out of the shower-room and he seemed distant—not moody, because he managed to reply adequately, even courteously, to the breakfast chatter, but he just wasn't with them.

Henrietta's thoughts were wry. Johnny Carruthers kids himself. He wants a wife, yes. A helpmeet sort of wife, not a true-love, soul-of-my-soul, flesh-of-my-flesh sort of wife, but a pleasant companion, adaptable, a good sport, slightly adventurous. So I seem ideal. But one mention of Deirdre and he's back in a world of dreams, longing for the unattainable. Henrietta was glad Madame was not up for breakfast. Dearly as she loved her, this morning she would just be a reminder of an hour that had been filled with hope ... and its quenching.

Not that there was time to brood. There never was at Dragonshill. Meals loomed largely in their minds. Mountain men had mountain appetites and they were forever at the ovens, putting in huge roasts and casseroles, cooking two or three puddings at once, stocking up biscuit and cake tins that seemed to empty overnight.

Penny said, 'I love cooking, and of course I was trained for just that, but time is my bugbear, it just

97

won't stretch. I no sooner see two or three days clear when I think I'll stock up with really huge bakings, when some emergency or other comes along and blots up my time. I had a real onslaught two weeks ago when Verona came and took my two back with her to Four Peaks and I cooked all those huge Christmas cakes and puddings in a sort of non-stop effort—some for Christmas itself, but most for the celebrations. And I did a huge stack of shortbread and gingernuts. I'm so thankful for things that keep.

'I had planned, however, to cook a heap of cookies—biscuity things, to put into bags in the deep-freeze, but we had extra help for the lambing—I do wish we lambed earlier like they can on the plains and the coast—and it somehow never got done.'

Henrietta said, 'How about my concentrating on that? I can't achieve the magnificent cakes you do, but even at the flat I did all my own baking. I'm not too bad on biscuits. What say I stock up the deep-freeze, then after Christmas I could whack up a whole lot of those biscuits you put in the fridge in rolls and bars, and just slice them thinly and bake them a day or two before they're needed? How about that?'

Penny flung her arms about her. 'It would be marvellous. I'm looking forward to the plaque-laying immensely. It seems to set the seal on Dragonshill's history, this event, while Grand'mère is still with us, but I admit it takes a lot of coping with and I don't want Gregory and Charlotte feeling I have no time for them, poor lambs. Charles has ordered tins and tins of shop biscuits, but in the main I want to conform as much as possible with the idea of the self-supporting homestead and the pioneer fare of the early days.'

'We'll do it,' said Henrietta, donning a huge white apron and going in search of the recipe books.

Johnny came into the kitchen looking less taciturn. 'Henrietta, you can get out of that voluminous garment pronto. Charles wants you out with us. We're going round the sheep. He says every hand counts.'

'Well, he'll have to do without my pair,' said Henrietta firmly, bringing the strings round to the front and tying them firmly. 'Every hand counts here too. Penny likes to be outside as much as anyone, and if I assist her, she won't be too worn out before the big day.'

This left Johnny with nothing to say, but Penny said hastily, 'I'm sure it could wait a day or two, Henrietta. It would do you good to——'

'It would do us all good to know the cupboards were full. We'll play afterwards when we've earned our leisure.'

Johnny said, 'I don't reckon you'll get any till it's all over. For two or three weeks after Christmas, in the hottest time of year, you'll be flat out with final preparations. It will take you—I mean you women—a week to recover from the festivities, and by then there'll be precious little of the school holidays left, then down to schoolroom grind. Besides, it's not play—we're——'

'No, and I mean no. I'm paid to help Penny. You sound as if you think I'll be immured once school starts. You know darned well they start lessons at eight here, so they can get plenty of sun after school before it sets behind the mountains—they have a very short dinnertime and we're finished with lessons by one-thirty and are outside then. Now scram. Penny, whoever wore this apron? Have you got a smaller?'

Penny started to laugh. 'It belongs to Mrs. Richards. She's ... er ... sort of robust.'

Johnny grinned too. 'She's not so much robust as plain busty, Penny darling. You can't possibly wear that, Henrietta, unless you ...'

He scooped up a folded roller towel Penny had put out to replace a soiled one and stuffed it into the front of the bulging apron ... stepped back and surveyed his handiwork, while Henrietta tugged at it.

His eyes were dancing. 'Vision of the future ... Henrietta Carruthers at the turn of the century ... with an ample bosom on which to rock her grandchildren to sleep.'

Henrietta pulled the towel out, flourished a rolling-pin in his direction, and he dodged out of the kitchen.

Penny said thankfully, 'He's himself again. He was so quiet at breakfast. It's unnatural in Johnny. I thought Grand'mère had really put her foot in it last night. Though surely he's got over Deirdre by now.'

Henrietta said calmly, 'He hasn't, you know. He only thinks he has. There are people like that. I'm another. We're dopes. We can't help it, though, we're made that way. I'm a one-man woman. Johnny Carruthers is a one-woman man.'

Penny pulled a face. 'I just don't believe it. I—Oh, my gosh, I've just realized something. You can't have noticed it either. He didn't say Henrietta King, he said Henrietta Carruthers! Then he *can't* be a one-man woman! Henrietta, it's a long time since——' She stopped. There were limits to what even Penny Beau-donais-Smith could get away with.

Henrietta finished it for her in a dead-flat voice. 'A long time since Godfrey died. Penny, Johnny and I are the only unattached ones here, and I'm twenty-nine and he's thirty-three, and all you dear people are so happily wed, you can't imagine one can achieve a certain happiness even in single state. It's going to make us very uncomfortable if we're thrown at each other's heads all the time.'

Penny looked mulish. 'Henrietta, *I* didn't tack Carruthers on to your name—Johnny did. He did it very naturally. So it looks as if you're embedded in his subconscious.'

Henrietta snorted. 'Embedded in his subconscious! He did it deliberately. I could choke him. He's so set on getting his own way he'll play you all up, use anybody and everybody just to get his own way.' She turned and seized a sifter with an air of one putting a thankful period to an uncomfortable conversation.

But Penny said, '*Get his own way!* Then that means he's asked you to——'

Henrietta sighed deeply. 'Penny, I turned Johnny

down four years ago. By letter. I turned him down again in Wellington, recently. No second-bests for me. It works with some. I've known several instances of first-loves being nothing more than infatuation, and a second and deeper attachment following that didn't have half the fireworks, but lasted. But it isn't like that with us.'

Charles could have told Henrietta that Penny rarely gave up. 'I didn't mean your feeling for Godfrey was infatuation. But I don't think he'd ever expected you to go the rest of your life alone. Life *must* be long and lonely—and you had so pitifully little. And if you feel that a second marriage could seem disloyal, to his memory, and to the Kings, you're quite wrong. Queenie and Mike would love to see you married again, and they would be glad to think you married someone who had known and loved Godfrey too. And Johnny needs you. It's such a waste of your talents. *You* wouldn't be afraid to follow your man. You're as intrepid as Grand'mère was.'

Henrietta said, 'Penny, I'm not thinking of Godfrey. Johnny deludes himself. Did you see his face last night when Deirdre's name was mentioned? No, of course you didn't. The rest of you were all too busy trying *not* to look at him. He recovered himself almost immediately and simply looked impassive, but I got just a glimpse. By the time she gets here Johnny will have such control of himself the mask won't slip again. Yes, he needs a wife, and—being Johnny—he thought he could pick up the bits of my life and fit them together again for me. But a jig-saw's not much good if some bits are missing. Something went out of my life when— oh, never mind. That's past. So I'd be awfully grateful if nobody continues matchmaking. It wouldn't work. I want this to be the happiest of times, for Madame's celebrations. No complications ... so leave it alone, will you, Penny? Possibly I've missed something in life, but lots of women have faced widowhood and come to terms with it. It *can* happen that one love is enough for a lifetime.'

Penny said in a small, unhappy voice, 'But I still wish Grand'mère hadn't invited Deirdre. It could be, of course, that at last she's getting forgetful. We'll just have to humour her.'

'Yes, nothing must mar her big day. And perhaps, as she has lived so much longer than any of us, she's more tolerant of Deirdre.'

'I believe she is—she must be—but what I don't like is——'

'Go on ... don't stop there. None of this affects me, you know.'

'Well, you've made it plain it doesn't, only it makes me uneasy. Deirdre——'

'I hate unfinished sentences and second thoughts. Deirdre what——?'

'You know how she loved hitting the high spots? She's always gone on his trips with Rodney Santos. *He* doesn't go into remote jungles and mountains where women would have to rough it. Oh, no. He goes to New York, Los Angeles, Sydney, Hongkong. Can't you just see Deirdre in the glittering life of Hongkong ... she'd never even notice those crowded, pitiful refugee quarters. And Singapore, she once told Hilary, is her favourite. Deirdre goes there with him if it's only for a week. And it's two months this time. You see, quite apart from Rodney's fabulous job, he inherited money.

'It worries me that she stayed in New Zealand. Why? Not that I'd have cared had not Grand'mère invited her here. Johnny's not the sort to go to Christchurch and hang round a married woman—at least I don't think he is—but here, with Johnny the only unattached male around ... oh, I feel sick!'

So did Henrietta. And sorry too, for Johnny. His old feeling for Deirdre, apparently only dormant, she thought as she recalled his face last night, could flare up again into something that could spoil his life. A wild regret washed over Henrietta, submerging her momentarily. Perhaps if she had been kinder to

Johnny, if she hadn't been so forthright, so definite, an obvious attachment between them, however lukewarm, might have protected him ... but ...

Penny said brightly, 'Oh, hullo, Grand'mère, I didn't realize you were up.'

It was a miracle Henrietta's baking turned out so well, because it was hard to keep her mind on it, to keep the past at bay.

Oddly enough, it was Godfrey who occupied her thoughts most. It had been so badly timed, all of it. She had had a feeling at the time that life was sucking them up like cardboard boxes drawn up into a whirlwind, and tossing them hither and thither, and they had just had to stay where they landed.

There had been that lovely spring when somehow, miraculously, she and Johnny had been at Pukewhetu together. It had been some time since their holidays had coincided. Henrietta had been sure the absence had made a difference, that Johnny might begin to see her, not as a tomboy sister, but as a woman. She had been purposely a little distant, wary, not so ready as of old to get into old clothes and help with the dipping, the feeding-out, the drafting. She had had before her exactly three weeks, when she could shake off being a schoolma'am or a sort of farm rouseabout, and revel in being a woman.

But less than a week had passed before Deirdre, supposedly recovering from a broken heart, had come up to stay with the Llewellyns, Verona's aunt and uncle. How speedily that heart had mended

She had deliberately set out for Johnny's scalp, and had succeeded. Henrietta had gone back to her teaching position in Christchurch numbed and had had the painful experience of having Johnny in Christchurch for weeks, the brief weeks of his engagement to Deirdre. Two days after it was broken Johnny flew out to his father who was in Malaya.

Christmas had been a joyless affair. Henrietta had gone to Pukewhetu as usual, hoping against hope

Johnny might fly in. Godfrey had been wonderful. Henrietta had been sure he knew. There hadn't been as much as a card from Johnny, though he'd sent the Kings presents.

They got a combined letter at New Year. He had mentioned future contracts on which his father would need him. Those contracts had stretched ahead of Henrietta like a limitless desert. They would keep John Carruthers away from New Zealand for years.

She'd had to face it. Johnny had simply pulled up the tent-pegs and gone out of her life for good. She'd had an idea that had he stayed in New Zealand they might have come together. But they might never meet again. He was going to be in such remote corners of the earth, they had no chance of running into each other, of finding it good.

Certainly she aimed to travel now she had completed her training and paid back her bond in three years of teaching service in her own country, but she wouldn't go to those sort of countries. Johnny must never suspect she carried a torch for him.

In London, where she would eventually meet up with her parents, New Zealanders were always running across each other at New Zealand House, or in Earl's Court or the Bank of New Zealand, but Johnny would be deep in swampy jungles, he could be in Nepal, in Korea, in Indonesia. You could only meet a man there if you pursued him.

But there were other things in life besides love. Henrietta loved teaching and in the classroom you got to grips with life. There was always Pukewhetu for the holidays, and Queenie, and Mike and Douglas ... and Godfrey, who never changed. Godfrey who never put a finger to the sore spots, probing. He was always there when you needed him.

So that January Henrietta appeared to have fun. Pukewhetu wasn't remote like Dragonshill, no river cut it off suddenly from all the festivities of the Mackenzie Country. There were parties and dances galore, picnics and trips to Timaru. None seemed gayer than Henrietta.

The night before she returned to Christchurch, Godfrey asked her to marry him. Henrietta almost consented, then, aware of an emotional pit yawning before her, drew back and told Godfrey she could not decide.

Godfrey, true to type, accepted her hesitation as something very natural for a girl. Marriage was for ever and one must be sure, even as he was. He told her he'd be in Christchurch in March, and would come for her answer then.

It had been a terrific surprise, almost a shock, when he came and mentioned that he'd been in town the best part of a week without coming to see her. Though she had been going to refuse him and had an uncomfortable idea he'd guess why.

She'd gazed at him. He didn't look well. Godfrey's features were as finely cut as a cameo and his hair looked darker ... or was it that his face was paler? She was more aware than before of the bone structure of his face. How like his father he had become!

He'd been so matter-of-fact it had been throat-constricting. He'd been having tests all week. It was leukaemia, of a type about which little was known as yet. They thought a year. She could forget all about what he'd asked her. He'd even smiled as he said, 'I'm sure I couldn't face a lifetime without you, Henrietta, but I can make out for a year.'

But it hadn't been that long. He went into Timaru Hospital, but they told Queenie he could be out of hospital for spells provided he could stay in Timaru. Queenie was torn between two places, Timaru and Tekapo. Whenever Godfrey went back to hospital she slipped up to Pukewhetu to set things in order in a couple of hectic days, for Mike and Douglas, living on the edge of her nerves, longing to get back to Timaru again.

Henrietta took a relieving position in a Timaru school and was there when Queenie wasn't, at visiting hours. There was a false improvement, then the doctor's warning that Queenie must slow her pace. During that time Henrietta asked Godfrey if he would marry her; that she would like that much to remember, that they could rent a flat in Timaru, then she would be with him when he had his spells out of hospital. She would not wait till he had the next one. A wedding at the flat might be too exciting. It could be in hospital, then, a week later, rested and restored, he could come to her.

Immediately the strain left Queenie and Mike. Godfrey lay in bed happily planning their home-to-be, with Henrietta taking in samples of curtaining and carpeting, and catalogues of furniture—all to preserve an illusion of happiness.

They brought his treasures down from the Hill of the Stars, set them up in a flat that was chosen with an eye to comfort and easy nursing, arranged for his own minister from Fairlie to perform the ceremony.

Henrietta told herself that Godfrey had brought her all the happiness she had known ... a home for her school holidays, Queenie ... Johnny. So for what time he had left, she would do all in her power to give him happiness. She knew she did it in a strength not her own. And the night before Godfrey was to come home to her, he had died in his sleep, smiling.

Through it all her greatest comfort was that she had made him happy those last few days, that he had not lingered but had gone as he would have wished to have gone, without fuss, and without too much anguish for them, and that she had helped Queenie and Mike when they had needed it most.

But when she found Godfrey had left a will in her favour, she demurred. Had cried out that she wanted no financial benefit for what she had done. It had taken Uncle Mike to convince her that they wanted her to have Godfrey's money.

He'd said, gently, 'Godfrey wanted this. He said he'd not much to leave you in personal happiness and memories, but that he'd like to think you had enough money now to go to your parents whenever you wanted to. He even said,' Mike had paused, then gone on, 'that you might like to take a trip to see Johnny some time.'

But there had been one thing even Godfrey hadn't been able to give her ... the confidence to do such a thing. And later Johnny's written proposal had only infuriated and insulted her. Suddenly her thoughts faltered. It *was* an insult to offer a woman second-best. It had been cold and unfeeling. Because Henrietta knew that if only Johnny had pretended he truly loved her, that his feeling for Deirdre had been nothing but infatuation, she would have married him.

Henrietta went on stamping out spicy German biscuits into circles and managed to discipline her stampeding thoughts again. Perhaps it was as well that Grand'mère had made her *faux pas*, because it had revealed to Henrietta in the nick of time that Johnny still cared for Deirdre. Last night she had been in danger of softening.

The men were frantically busy, with the sheep as well as with the bridge approach from the Tekapo side. A huge gang of men had arrived for that, setting up camp in Ministry of Works huts on the Llewellyn property, and it was an unusual sight to see such huge material being manoeuvred into place. Conditions were ideal, there had been an early thaw this year and consequently the river level wasn't changing much. Not that you could ever count on that, because here, close to the watersheds and the source of the river, it could be running bank to bank in three hours, with heavy rain.

Johnny explained they had problems just the same. 'If we had an electrical storm at the very time, say, we could be one side of the river, Grand'mère and all of us, and the official party stranded on the other. We'll just have to hope and pray.

'But we're arranging for helicopters if necessary, and Morwyn's plane, of course, but it would limit the numbers. And of course, flying conditions right in the Alps here are not always ideal. However, we'll worry about that when it comes. One thing I do hope, and that is that on the Sunday before the ceremony, the special thanksgiving in the Church of the Good Shepherd at Tekapo can take place.'

Queenie and Uncle Mike were coming across to Dragonshill for tea on Christmas evening and staying the night. Otherwise Henrietta would have gone to them for Christmas, as Douglas would be at Marianne's place and Henrietta did not want the Kings to spend Christmas alone.

She thought she sensed a shade of disapproval in Johnny's eyes as she said this. So she added: 'After all, Johnny, I *am* a King.'

His response was instant. 'Of course you are. Can I ever forget that?'

She frowned. 'What do you mean by that?'

'I'm fully aware, Henrietta, that you never forget them.'

She said, rather wearily, 'Johnny, I don't feel under a burden of gratitude to them. It's simply that I love them. The King family brought me most of the happiness I've known.'

He said, rather roughly, which puzzled her, 'Of course you aren't under a burden of gratitude. You gave everything you could to their son. And quite apart from what you did for him, Queenie looks on you as a daughter, always did. She's so happy with you here. She sort of came to life when you arrived.'

Henrietta said, 'I expect she feels it's a link. Would you mind passing those pots of raspberry jam up to me? Bring the whole tray through, would you? I'd like to put them in the store-room.'

She went through, Johnny following her. He handed them up two by two, as she stood on the top of the steps. She began to come down. Johnny put a hand across her knees and stopped her. 'Sit down,' he commanded, exerting pressure. 'It's all right. You won't tip over. I've got you.'

She sat. She knew better than to struggle with him, when she inevitably came off worst. They were fairly low steps and this brought her on a level with him. He put an arm firmly across the top of her knees. 'That's better. You can't fly from me without crashing. Now what's the matter? You've been avoiding me ever since we went up the Rock of Ages.'

She was very calm. 'Have I? You've always been good at imputing motives to people. And you're far from being omniscient. I've been busy, I suppose. Penny would run herself ragged if we didn't watch her. It's not easy organizing a big affair like this, even if everyone will contribute, so——'

'So you've been far too tired, or so you've said, every night, to come out and walk with me. Yet the nights I don't, you go out and play the most exhausting and tireless games of tennis with Arene or Walter, I've ever witnessed. So I'm forced to believe you're just——'

He was interrupted. 'You're forced to believe that I just don't want to go with you. You could be right. You're still a thrawn de'il, Johnny, as old Eliza McCraw would say, aye wanting what you can't have, and for very little other reason.'

The blue eyes narrowed. His face was an inch from hers. 'You said *I* was always imputing motives to other people. Ever heard of people in glasshouses, etc., etc.? And you ought to know my reasons are much more firmly based than that.' His arms were slowly creeping round her. 'You do this sort of thing with Queenie too. I know Queenie loves you for yourself, not just because you were Godfrey's wife. She always did. It was never a foregone conclusion that you should marry Godfrey. In fact——' he stopped.

Henrietta just wouldn't ask him what he was going to say. She sat, looking—in the most maddening fashion imaginable—as if she was just enduring this because if she struggled, on these steps, she'd fall, and it would be most undignified.

He said, 'The old Henrietta would have fought like a tiger. You aren't half as much fun as you used to be.'

She shrugged. 'Not worth the effort. You could always outrun me, out-bully me, use your brute strength to prove to yourself how superior you were, how right you were.'

It didn't succeed, as she had hoped, in making him let her go.

He said easily enough, his face close to hers, 'Well, if you aren't going to give me the fun of the chase, I'll take my fun another way, slowly and deliberately.'

He bent to kiss her. Thoughts raced through Henrietta's mind. Men were so different from women. Even though Johnny's true love wouldn't have him, he was thoroughly enjoying this. That was what made it possible for him to contemplate marriage with her. He would never feel for her what he'd once felt for Deirdre, yet this ... what Henrietta could give him, would be better than nothing. Bitterness swept over Henrietta and in a moment the sheer magic of Johnny's arms about her, Johnny's lips on hers, was gone.

And for once this blind, hulking lump of arrogance knew it. He lifted his head and stared at her, his eyes raking hers. He said, furiously, 'You're the most abominable creature I've ever known! You're—oh, I don't know what you are! Talk about cold and frigid!'

Henrietta came to life. The peat-brown eyes blazed at him. 'I am *not* frigid! How could *you* possibly know? Men! Talk about vanity ... just because a woman doesn't respond, they dub her frigid, cold. Anything rather than admit to themselves something damaging to the lordly male ego ... that if a woman doesn't respond to a man, it simply means she doesn't care for *that particular man*! Not that she's some kind of biological freak! How dare you!'

It had the oddest effect upon him. One moment he'd

gone quite white, the next his face was suffused with the colour of anger.

'Of course I dare. And I'd a damned sight rather have you like this than an iceberg...'

Henrietta thought he was going to kiss her again, and suddenly she was afraid, anger evaporating and leaving her empty and vulnerable.

He saw the sparks die down and fear take its place and suddenly he said, 'Oh, sorry, Henrietta darling. You're right, I'm an ill devil to cross. I go the wrong way about everything. There, there, never mind.' He held her against him, her face against his thin shirt, his hand stroking her hair. Henrietta stayed there, bewildered, yet comforted. She'd never, never understand John Carruthers!

She sensed he'd lifted his head, so she lifted hers too, to find him gazing in the direction of the door behind her and smiling a little. She turned apprehensively and saw Madame Beaudonais framed in the doorway. She was leaning a little on her stick and looking very amused.

Her eyes twinkled as she met Henrietta's embarrassed ones.

'This is not a romantic age, I fear,' Madame complained. 'Me, I should want the moon shining over Erebus or the little paths that run through the larch wood. But then I am an old, outdated woman. But I cannot, no, I cannot see romance in bags of onions and sacks of flour. Johnny, I thought better of you. 'But nevertheless, I am ver', ver' happy for you, *mes enfants*.' And she walked away.

Henrietta put her head in her hands. 'Look what you've done now,' she moaned.

CHAPTER SIX

HENRIETTA could have smacked Johnny when he burst out into gusts of uncontrollable laughter.

She said, distantly, 'I see nothing to laugh at. It's becoming a fixed idea with Madame. We'll have to think of some way to convince her it's not—not like that.'

Johnny sobered up, took her chin in one hand, and turned her face up to him so that she had to meet his eyes. 'Would you really take away that happy look in the eyes of a woman a hundred years old, Henrietta? It would be like giving a child a toy and taking it back five minutes later.'

She bit her lip, 'Yes,' she said unhappily, 'But if we let her go on thinking that——'

'Henrietta, Madame isn't exactly going to announce we are engaged, is she? There's nothing dim about Madame. But we can scarcely go and explain that I was kissing you because we were fighting, can we? This is something between the two of us. Our lives got snarled up, didn't they? and are hopelessly entangled.'

Henrietta's brows drew together. 'They aren't, you know ... you only think they are. After all, you can't browbeat me into a second-rate marriage. We'll let it go. And I think you could be wrong about Madame's faculties. She'd never have invited Deirdre here if her memory hadn't been failing a little.'

Johnny didn't look put out. Nor was there a hint of the emotion Henrietta had glimpsed in his face when Madame had dropped her clanger the other night. In fact he grinned. 'Jealous, are you? I'd like to think so.'

Henrietta gave an exasperated sound. 'You must be clean mad. But it seemed odd. Look, I'm going to be as devastatingly frank as you are. I can't remember Madame being fond enough of Deirdre all those years ago, that she'd even want to have her here for her big day. I mean Deirdre came up here that spring, did her damage and departed. Things have never been quite the same again. I'm not going to pretend I liked her. And I know Madame didn't either. So she must be losing her grip a little. She must have forgotten all that happened.'

If Johnny didn't resent any of this, he hid it well.

He said, mildly for him, 'Perhaps Madame has become more tolerant. People mellow with age. So Madame must have mellowed more than most, as she's lived so much longer. And perhaps she thinks Deirdre will be lonely with Rodney away, and that she, too, may have changed.'

Henrietta reflected that leopards weren't supposed to change their spots and that this one was certainly a man-eater.

Then she jerked her head back to take in what he was saying now.

He was saying, 'In fact Madame knows very well that Deirdre *has* changed.'

'What can you mean?'

'I mean that when Madame spent a fortnight in Christchurch with Nancy Hipatea—Verona went to visit Nancy and took Madame with her—the old lady took it into her head to go to see Deirdre and Rodney.'

Henrietta blinked. 'Does Penny know? She's not said anything.'

'No, she doesn't.'

'Then how did *you* know, John Carruthers?'

'Deirdre and Rodney told me.'

Henrietta sat very still. It seemed a long time before she could even draw a breath.

She said, finally, 'When?'

'When I was in New Zealand earlier. When I came for the first time about the bridge.'

He'd seen Deirdre. And Rodney. And hadn't even

bothered to come to see Henrietta! Oh, he'd said he had his reasons for not having told her he'd been at Dragonshill, but that was probably a lot of eyewash. And what in heaven's name was he looking so amused for?

So she said coldly, 'With all your faults, Johnny, your tantalizing ways—your incomprehensible actions —I never thought of you as a liar. Why did you pretend you didn't know if they had a family or not the other night?'

'Because it seemed to me that Madame must have a reason for concealing her visit to Deirdre.'

Henrietta put a hand to her head; it was beyond her. Then she managed, 'Then you should know if Deirdre has changed or not.'

'Oh, I know all right. She *has* changed—very much for the better. She'd just been hopelessly spoiled, you know. Rodney didn't continue that. There had been nothing to develop her character, no adversity of any kind. And what Deirdre wanted, she took, but——'

Henrietta said, 'You might as well go on. But what?'

'It's hard to define. There's definitely a change. She has more depth now. To hark back to Madame's scrapbooks would explain it best, out of that "Said About Women" column. I thought I'd learned a lot about women from that, and I had. But not about you, Henrietta. I still don't know what makes you tick.'

She said coldly, 'We were talking about Deirdre,'

'Oh, yes. This snippet said that no woman was worth very much until she had been through a great deal of sadness, a great deal of wanting that which she could not get.'

Henrietta dropped her eyes, letting her beautifully curved lids shutter their expression against Johnny's gaze. Yes, she was jealous of Deirdre. Deirdre wanting that which she could not get ... Deirdre sad, forlorn. How appealing Deirdre would be in a sad mood. Henrietta could only guess. She'd always wanted to have her cake and eat it too. Falling in love with John Carruthers, but not enough to follow him into the barren, tough places of the earth, she had married Rodney Santos, older than Johnny thought not by much, a city man with a glamorous future, visiting regularly the capitals of the world. Yet she was still, evidently, looking back wistfully to the man she had given up for an easier way of life.

Johnny said impatiently, 'You're retreating into your shell again, your secret world. Come out of it. Aren't you going to comment on that? Doesn't it matter to you at all?'

'Not particularly. I'm not really interested in Deirdre. She's not my type. Not a woman's woman, only a man's woman. That's not meant to be catty, Johnny. It's just a statement of fact, though you'll probably never believe it.'

'I know you aren't catty. You've not got it in you. I grew up with you, remember?'

'Thanks. At least you've granted me the privilege— and the relief—of being as frank as yourself, something men don't always allow women. It's the oddest thing. Men say they don't like subterfuge, yet it's a well-known fact that men don't like women running other women down. I feel much better for saying I didn't like Deirdre. I admit she was attractive—very—but I've very little patience with women who won't follow their men, not only into the backblocks, either, like Madame, because some women find it just as hard to follow their men into political careers or big business. The women who are shy, who'd rather by far face swamp and jungle, with a bridge-building husband, or take to the solitudes of the high-country, than face the boring and interminable ceremonies and gruelling political campaigns of public life. I met so many of them when I was with the Department, and I admired them tremendously.'

'Then you think that could be a test of whether a woman truly loved a man, or not? That if she did, she would be ready to go with him wherever he was going, and whatever he did?'

No doubt it was turning the knife in the wound; Deirdre had, after all, turned him down for just this, but he'd asked, and he seemed to want a fair answer.

So she said, 'Let's put it this way. It's quite easy to turn a man down, making his way of life an excuse, if you don't really love him. If you do, nothing would hold you back.'

Oh, she was being cruel, but it was far better for John Carruthers to face facts, because Henrietta just couldn't bear to see him drawn into Deirdre's toils again.

Johnny walked to the door, looked back at her. 'You're quite good at taping other people's lives, Henrietta. It must come from being in a Government Department so long. But what about yourself? What's your ideal existence?'

Henrietta looked puzzled. 'You said we grew up together, so you must know. It's so simple. My ideal existence is *this*. Dragonshill and the Hill of the Stars. All this fierce, wild Mackenzie Country. This is *my* venue. But if I loved a man I'd follow him into either the jungle of the political world or the ends of the earth. It's as easy as that.'

He smiled crookedly, one hand on the door-frame, and shook his head. 'It's not, you know. Not easy.' And was gone.

Henrietta didn't know what this conversation had achieved, except for deepening her conviction that Johnny still cared for Deirdre. But she thought she knew why he wanted to marry. It was because Johnny Carruthers held marriage in too high a regard to play around with another man's wife even if, as seemed likely, she had played on his sympathies.

She heard him coming back.

'Yes?' she asked.

'Pity you'd not voiced those opinions to Rodney Santos instead of to me.'

Her voice was almost shrill with surprise. 'Why?'

'Because I've a pretty good idea that was why Rodney asked me to visit them. He was observing Deirdre and me together. I think he's always wondered if she chose a way of life rather than the man.' And he went away again.

Henrietta felt more than ever confused. There was only one thing she was sure of, and that was that it was a great pity Madame Beaudonais had invited Deirdre to Dragonshill when Rodney was absent.

Henrietta found dinner an ordeal. Johnny was in high spirits—something that always made her apprehensive. And Madame's eyes held a blessing in them every time her eyes rested on the pair of them, sitting together half-way down the large dining-table.

To Henrietta's sharpened perceptions, it seemed as if it would be evident to all. And Johnny took wicked advantage of it by being extremely proprietorial with Henrietta, something that couldn't fail to be noticed by everybody.

Penny revealed this by being over-casual. Charles, an uncomplicated man, merely beamed on them occasionally, in the manner of a family man who likes peace and harmony after ructions, and as Brigid and Judy were having dinner at Dragonshill, they were irritatingly giggly, and Henrietta was sure Grand'mère must have said something—perhaps nothing definite, but enough to make them outrageously enthusiastic about a possible love-affair between their elders. Most teenagers reacted like this. Henrietta simply didn't know how to handle any of them.

Johnny said, when the interminable meal was over and he stood up to help clear away the dishes, 'Oh, by the way, Charles, I'll be away tomorrow. I was speaking to Matt Greenwood on the phone this afternoon, and Joanna chipped in and asked me and Henrietta over for the day tomorrow. Penny says she can spare Henrietta and all the rivers are low, so we can take the horses. You can have Ebony Maid, Henrietta, and I'll take Copper Boy.'

Henrietta knew it was useless to protest. Anyway, it would get her away from the assumptions and match-makings of Dragonshill and into an atmosphere that would be natural and friendly, with no embarrassing moments.

It was a glorious morning. Henrietta wore ribbed dark green cotton trews and an apple-green shirt open at the throat, and had slipped an Alice band in green over her hair to keep it out of her eyes. Her peaty-brown eyes showed tawny glints in them where the sun shone on the two riders, striking dazzling lights from the snow-pockets, and her hair was a shining cap, darkly brown.

As they came up out of the first stream of the Awatipua, the river they must ford to get to Heronscrag, the Greenwoods' sheep-station, with the many streams of the Pawerawera safely behind them, Johnny said, 'It's an idyllic day, Henrietta, let's keep it that way, shall we?'

She bent forward to caress Ebony Maid's curved neck. 'Why not? It's mostly when other people are around, with the pressure they bring to bear upon us, that we fight. After all, Matthew and Joanna Green-wood are hardly likely to want to force the same issue—to matchmake. Matchmaking is a real menace.'

There was a smile in his voice. 'Yes, at times. Though perhaps it's just that happily married people can't resist it because they know all the emotions are double-strength when shared. But in our case——'

When he didn't seem inclined to finish it, she prompted him.

'In our case ...?'

He laughed. 'I said we'd keep this day idyllic. I mustn't put a flint to the tinder.'

Curiosity got the better of her. 'I hate unfinished sentences. If I promise not to take you up on it will you finish it?'

'Okay. In our case these matchmakers might have been more successful had they adopted the technique of that jingle of the old-time autograph books. Remember?

> *"He was warned against the woman,*
> *She was warned against the man,*
> *And if that won't make a marriage,*
> *Then there's nothing else that can!"*

'What say you to that, Henrietta?'

Their eyes met, the blue and the brown. She remembered her promise, said easily, 'Yes, it might have worked. But before a person can warn, there has to be something unknown by the other one. From childhood on, our lives were an open book to each other—nothing to warn about.'

He said reflectively, 'Yes, no mystery. I wonder what would have happened had we not met till we were ... say twenty-four and twenty-eight? What impact might we have made upon each other?'

Henrietta shrugged. 'Perhaps none at all. It's the Deirdres of the world who make the impact.'

'Watch it, Henrietta, keep it idyllic—and uncontroversial. A fellow's allowed one infatuation, surely.'

Infatuation. The very first hint that it might have been only that. Much better than saying, 'I should know, none better, that sometimes one particular person has a place in one's heart that no one else can take.'

She said, touching her heel to Ebony Maid's flank, 'That was rather mean of me. I'll leave Deirdre out of it. Tell me, Johnny, what is Joanna like? I know and like Matt, of course.'

Johnny's voice warmed. 'Oh, you're bound to like her. She's ideal for Matt. And talk about game ... just imagine, she was private secretary to a T.V. star, Maria Delahunt, no less, and had led about the most glamorous life a girl could lead. She got stranded in the

Waimihi river-bed just before that colossal snowstorm last winter, had never done a thing beyond making her bed in all her life and had to look after Matt and the men and his cousin's children. Matt must have been a fast worker. He had her promise to marry him before the snow melted and the river went down. It takes some men years to browbeat a woman into marrying them.'

Henrietta laughed. 'The schoolma'am in me makes me comment on what a very badly-constructed sentence that is ... you've got your plurals and singulars all mixed up. And I don't find it very surprising that they decided things so quickly. No family complications, no snarling up of relationships, and blessed solitude. The time, the place, *and* the loved one. It must have been love at first sight.'

'Don't you believe it. Joanna thought Matt was engaged, you see, and they'd got off on the wrong foot from the very first moment. Matt blew his top because she'd ventured across the river ... and rising waters caught her car going back. He and she only just got out of it, you know.'

'No, I didn't know. Tell me, Johnny, will it work? I mean, a girl with a background like that!'

'It will work. You'll know that from the moment you see them together. The bond between them is something that—well, it lifts the heart. She loves the mountains and had always hated social life. I suppose heredity counts for something. She's Henry Dean's greatniece, you see—the one who owned Heronscrag when he was a young man. That's why Joanna was in the river-bed, taking photos to send back to him. And now he lives in Tekapo, and is married to Christine Dunmuirson. At least he lives there when they are not out at Heronscrag. Look out ... there's a dottrell's nest.'

Henrietta guided Ebony Maid round it. The sun poured down scorchingly and sparkled on the mica specks in some of the river-bed stones, tumbled down from glaciers in the Alps. The outline of the mountains against the cerulean sky was like something sculptured in marble by a master craftsman. Johnny was whistling in his inimitable manner ... switching from one tune to another in the most skilful and fascinating way ... a bar or two of *Edelweiss*, a verse of *Danny Boy*, a couple of lines of *My Love is like a Red, Red Rose* ... then the gaiety of *Funiculi, Funicula* ... Henrietta felt contentment seeping into her. Dangerous, but sweet.

Because Johnny was here, and he was singing her summer in ... 'Sweet tangled tunes more golden than the first gold Summer day ...'

After they had forded the last stream of the Awatipua, the country changed a little; they skirted the shoulder of one of the mountains and came into a tiny gorge, threaded through by a stream, and with very steep sides. It was impassable after heavy rain, but made a short cut when low, as now. Johnny looked up at the sides as they took to the stream bed. 'Lovely and narrow ... this will be bridged too, some day. There are several places like this that could link the isolated homesteads. It will be years and years before it's attempted, of course.'

Henrietta knew a pang. They would not be Carruthers' bridges by then. He'd be on the other side of the world by the time it came to bridge these, probably. And what would she be doing? Just growing older ... perhaps teaching generations of children yet unborn.

They came up out of the gorge, turned east, and here as a change from treeless tussock stretches and windswept river-beds, was a pocket of bush tucked into a valley and leading down to the dreamy, iridescent waters of one of the smaller lakes, Moana-kotuku, the Lake of the Rare White Heron.

Johnny said, 'The New Zealand habit of calling this sort of terrain bush is ridiculous. I meet lots of chaps overseas who imagine it as low scrub, not tall beech forests like this.'

Henrietta nodded. 'I wonder how it came to be called just that? The pioneers called the native beech birch, didn't they? But you can see the reason for that. The leaves are tiny like birch leaves. Oh, I'd forgotten how beautiful Evergreen Valley is ... this mossy stream, and the host of tiny growths on every fallen stump and in the crevices of every living tree ... and the dragonflies ... look how their gauzy wings glint.'

Johnny turned in towards the greenness. 'We're going to have morning-tea here.'

He swung down and came towards her, putting out his hand.

She said, 'I can manage well enough myself, you know.'

His eyes met hers squarely. 'Sure you can. Just as women can open doors and cross busy roads by themselves—but aren't they also supposed to enjoy attentions from men, and mutter about chivalry being dead if they don't get them?'

She grinned, looking down on him. 'You're dead right, we do.'

He put up his arms and as she came down into them, he said, 'Besides, it's so very enjoyable,' but did not take advantage of her nearness. And perversely, she wished he had.

They tethered the horses and Johnny took a flask and cookies from his saddle-bag. By mutual but unspoken consent they made for a spot where they had had a picnic years before. They splashed through the shallow stream in their boots and through an opening in the huge boulders that almost blocked the stream here. They had been tumbled down in time of storm when this purling brook had become a raging Alpine torrent; then they came out into the sunshine again, where a crystal clear pool reflected sky and clouds.

This was a place that belonged to only the two of them. They had stumbled upon it one day when Godfrey had been in Fairlie. Deirdre did not know of it, either. She didn't ride and there was no other access.

Henrietta, that first time they visited it, had been just fifteen. It had been the day she had first realized she loved him. Perhaps it had been nothing but hero-worship then, the feeling of a schoolgirl for a varsity student, but it had deepened and strengthened till it had become complete fidelity.

But she'd meant nothing to Johnny. Just Henrietta, madcap companion of the mountains. Yet there had been this kinship of spirit.

Then, as now, Johnny had led the way up to a pocket of shingle, barren-looking and inhospitable ground where, nevertheless, a clump of Mount Cook lilies had blossomed out of the greyness, each enormous buttercup-shaped flower waxen-white in its purity, and centred with bright orange and green stamens. He had picked a glossy saucer-shaped leaf filled with dew and given it to her to drink. Just as he did now. Henrietta gave herself up the sheer delight of the moment.

Johnny held up a finger, enjoining silence. There was music all about them. Birdsong sounding from the closely-clustered leaves, shallow waters singing over marble-smooth pebbles ground to a perfection of smoothness by aeons of glacial action, somewhere a cricket chirping, a hot, happy sound ... the countless rustlings of foliage, the wind murmuring down the valley walls, a thrush calling to his mate, her answer from another tree ... 'Not man-made music,' said Johnny, 'but the sort of music they heard in Eden.'

The sort of thing Johnny had so often said in pre-Deirdre days. Kindred things she had thought would inevitably build up to an awareness that they were two meant to be one. But it hadn't been that way. Might it happen again? Could she lull herself into a pain-killing belief that kinship of spirit and a real friendship could compensate for that tide of longing and desire that had been Johnny's feeling for Deirdre. The way Henrietta wanted to be loved.

They skirted the north-western shore of the Lake of the Kotoku, then came to the homestead in a glorious burst of gallop. That certainly blew all the cobwebs away, and inhibitions too. They by-passed the Heron-scrag air-strip and saw two figures come racing down to them.

Who could believe that this long-legged, tawny-haired girl had known the glittering world of the London stage? She seemed part and parcel of the mountains. She and Matthew Greenwood were running hand-in-hand. Henrietta found herself envying them fiercely.

'We thought you'd never come,' said Joanna eagerly. 'So this is Henrietta! Everybody talks about you here —especially Johnny. We've got the dinner all ready to serve. Only two of us today as the men are away up the Awatipua. And I think the dinner will be all right. You see, I'm only a learner cook. I'd never cooked in my life till I got marooned here last August. So every new recipe I try is fraught with perils. I've got a pine-apple soufflé in, but I baked an apple pie yesterday in case this flopped.'

'Gosh, had I known a soufflé was hanging in the balance,' said Johnny, 'I'd have brought my walkie-talkie with me and given you a pace-by-pace timetable of our arrival so you could have timed it perfectly. I'm all for getting a start on the dinner right now. It must be a full hour since we had any nourishment and I've a large frame to keep up.'

Matt said, 'Good, because we want to take you over to our thatched cottage afterwards ... and that's a fair way beyond the homestead.' He turned to Henrietta. 'Joanna fell in love with an old cottage that a previous owner and his wife built up one of the valleys running off the main Waimihi Valley. They used it for holidays when they couldn't get away off the place.

'I had it re-thatched with *raupo* reeds—it's the pride of our hearts.' He looked at Joanna and smiled, a brief smile that nevertheless held happy memories shared. 'We spent our honeymoon there. Not bad for a girl who was used to top-notch Continental service, was it,

Henrietta? Only lamplight and a Dover stove and the creek to draw water from. Though I did rig up a shower-room. A really spartan life ... snow water. We were married in October and it was still pretty cold.'

They rode to the cottage. Henrietta had never seen it in its tumbledown state, so the charm of its setting gripped her with delight. It was set back against the hill and faced east. A *rimu* tree stood guard over it, its green needles hanging pendulously like a piece of embroidery on a tapestry screen, many of the trees of New Zealand forest crowded about it—beeches, *matai*, *totara*, with ferns and mosses covering every inch of ground with prodigal verdure.

Lawyer vines hung in festoons from the branches and birdsong provided a sound background to the atmosphere of happiness that clung to the cottage, whose stones retained the lichens of the forest floor. The *raupo* thatch was stiffly new and honey-coloured, and there was a bright splash of colour where red and gold nasturtiums ran up beside the door to mingle with the thatch. Joanna had made two beds to hold the nasturtiums, filling them with rich moist earth from the bush, and edging them with river stones. 'The frost will cut them down early, but I don't care. They bloom brightly and briefly, and I love them.'

Matthew Greenwood had enlarged it to three rooms, a kitchen with a little black stove that stuck out into the room and had a pipe for the smoke, and a sitting-room with a floor made of flat split stones in soft greens, mauves and pinks, almost entirely covered with deer-skins, both red and virginian. There was a funny old-fashioned couch covered with skins too, a rocking-chair, a well-filled bookcase, and a wide grey stone fire-place with winking mica specks. It was piled with wood, ready for a match.

Henrietta had a vision of how it would have looked to these two when they forsook their Land-Rover for this sanctuary on their wedding-night. They would have made a ritual of lighting their first fire together as man and wife. Then later they would have retired to that room off it, through that open door. That one had a wooden floor, with lambskins, and a huge big old-fashioned padded quilt done in patchwork on the wide, low bed.

There was an old Scots kist in mahogany, with wooden knobs for handles to the drawers. It had a swing mirror-stand on top, and slightly yellowed crocheted mats threaded with blue ribbon. Its windows were latticed ones, framed with native clematis, and looked east. How wonderful to wake in that bed, with one's true love lying beside one, and to watch the wonder and magic of dawn on the Turehu Maunga, the Fairy Mountain, supposedly sacred to the light-skinned, ghostly people who inhabited the forests nearby.

She looked up from her pondering to find Johnny's eyes upon her. She dropped hers and blushed. How really stupid to imagine he could read her thoughts. Oh, how much easier it had been to disguise her feelings in Wellington. This life disarmed you, made you aware of your vulnerability, undermined your strong resolves.

Nevertheless, the day continued in a dreamlike fashion, and Matthew's and Joanna's happiness was infectious. They had an early tea, because even though it was high summer, they lost the sun early, close to the mountains as they were. Once the ball of that sun dropped westward behind the peaks, purple twilight enfolded this eastern side very quickly, and it was a long ride back.

So they came contentedly, if a little saddle-weary, to the stables at Dragonshill in the cool of the evening. Henrietta said quite simply and sincerely, 'Thank you, Johnny, for a lovely day—one to remember,' as he helped her down.

He smiled down on her. 'There are days like this, aren't there? When one can forget old unhappinesses and savour the present to the full. It was like that today with us, wasn't it, Henrietta?'

She nodded, content to have it that way.

He twinkled, 'I'm sure this is the time that new stars will be coming into view from here. It's my bounden duty to point them out to you. Your ignorance of the stars is appalling. How about it?'

She smiled back, 'All right by me.'

He said meaningfully, 'There are phases in all spheres of life—not just in the sphere of the stars. Okay, I'll unsaddle ... you go and shower. I'll shower in the outside one.'

But she took so long over her toilet that he was tubbed and in Madame's sitting-room long before she was.

He'd liked her in blue, he'd said that Sunday morning in Wellington, so she was wearing blue, a soft, silky thing, with a blurred pattern of different blues and purples that merged into each other. She had Johnny's pearls on and pearl earrings, pear-shaped, at her ears. And after gazing at Godfrey's diamond ring above her wedding ring for some time in her room, she had slipped it off and put it in her trinket box, and, instead, she was wearing Madame's pearl ring.

She was aware that her defences were crumbling. That Johnny Carruthers' second-best was still very good. That while he might never be able to give her what he had given Deirdre, they could build up a very fine life together. She had an idea she was going to let things take their course, offer no resistance.

So when she came in and Johnny smiled at her over everyone's heads, she smiled back quite unreservedly. It was heaven to feel like this ... at peace, and no longer distrustful.

Charles was telling Gregory a story, so no one spoke. Charles was a natural story-teller. Penny was keeping Charlotte quiet by threading beads for her, on a long string, and Madame was watching them with an indulgent smile on her face.

Johnny patted the seat beside him and obediently

Henrietta went to it. He indicated Gregory's intense face with a jerk of his head and whispered, 'What a listener! Watch him.'

Gregory had Charles's fair hair but Penny's brown eyes and he was sitting on the table edge, his feet on a chair, his hands between his knees, his eyes intent on his father's face. He nodded in agreement, or shook his head like a wise old owl at every dramatic point and shouted with laughter at the first hint of anything funny coming. A perfect family scene, and it was all still in the idyllic mood of the whole day. Johnny's hand came to hers, engulfing it, between them.

The children were put to bed and conversation became general. Johnny announced that he and Henrietta were going out later to see what new stars were dawning upon the Dragonshill horizon. Charles looked surprised and started to say something, but subsided quickly at a fierce glare from Penny and managed to say something quite feeble, to fill in. Henrietta wanted to laugh. She had a strong suspicion that there were no new stars due to appear, that Johnny and Charles and Penny knew that very well. But what did it matter?

Naturally they talked of their day at Heronscrag and of the Waimihi cottage.

Penny said, 'I think that was an ideal place for a honeymoon. Oh, it's all right, Carl, ours was ideal too ... we went back to the Sounds where we first met, but I mean this was ideal for Joanna and Matt. Had she always lived here she might have wanted to hit the high spots, but she came fresh to the high country and fell for the mountains, so spent the first days of her married life in the surroundings she loved best.'

Johnny had moved to a small table to knock out his pipe and refill it. He said in quite a matter-of-fact tone, 'As a point of interest, Henrietta, where did you and Godfrey spend your honeymoon? Or could you not travel far because of his illness?'

A complete and dumbfounded silence descended upon them all.

Finally, Penny broke it. 'But, Johnny, surely you knew they didn't have a honeymoon?'

He said quietly, 'Oh, sorry. Just stayed in the flat, did you, Henrietta?'

She swallowed, then said, her voice shaky, but with surprise rather than grief, 'Johnny—how did you not know? I mean, I thought everyone knew. I thought Queenie wrote you.' She swallowed again. 'We were married in hospital. But—but Godfrey never came out after the ceremony.'

There was an appalling crash and Madame's treasured pot-pourri bowl lay in fragments on the floral carpet.

Johnny stared down at it, almost as if he didn't know he'd done it, then he bent to pick up the pieces. 'Oh, I'm sorry, Madame. How on earth did I do that? How clumsy! I must've knocked it with my elbow. But it's Wedgwood, isn't it, so I should be able to replace it. I do hope it has no particular associations. I'll send for one.'

Madame said calmly, 'It is of no moment. Me, I am not a believer in crying over the spilt milk. No, indeed. And this room is far too cluttered. That is what comes of living over a century. After all, one collects far too much when one has gifts from a hundred Christmases and a hundred birthdays piled up round one.'

Henrietta came to help Johnny pick up the fragments, and the perfume of the long-forgotten roses of a thousand yesterdays came up to them. Penny brought the waste-paper basket across and they piled them into it.

Johnny seemed to be ill at ease for having broken Madame's bowl. He said abruptly, 'Well ... those stars. Better get a coat, Henrietta.'

She went along to her bedroom, fleetingly touched the lobes of her ears with white rose perfume, glanced briefly into her own mirrored eyes and smiled a little. An idyllic day, and an idyllic night was to follow. Johnny might have loved Deirdre madly once, but that was a long time ago, and perhaps there was more than one way to love.

Because she was sure, madly, gladly sure, that his clumsiness had been due to his sudden knowledge of what no one had told him before ... that it really mattered to John Carruthers that she and Godfrey had never been man and wife. So he must care. It wasn't just wanting the sort of wife who wasn't afraid to face the wildernesses with him.

Henrietta clipped a black-and-white checked cape about her throat and went down the hall quickly. Johnny had the back door open and was standing at it, right down the concrete porch. She sped towards him.

He turned a little, said, 'Right,' and they moved off into the starlit night.

He didn't speak. Henrietta hid a smile. For once Johnny Carruthers was tongue-tied. He wouldn't want to hurt her, wouldn't want to seem glad that she and Godfrey had never known fulfilment, so she would let him know that she quite understood, that she knew it was only natural, that were the positions reversed, she would feel the same. A gladness that Johnny could in any way have been jealous of Godfrey welled up in her.

When they were clear of the garden gate and the little larch path beyond it, she said, 'Are we going to the Rock of Ages, Johnny?'

He swung round on her, said, 'No, *not* to the Rock of Ages. This will be quite far enough, believe me. Made a fool of me, didn't you? I revealed my feelings in front of everyone. I can't think what I've seen in you! I must be a shocking judge of character—of women anyway—that's for sure. First Deirdre, then you!'

Henrietta put a hand to her head as if she'd been struck and took a step backwards. 'But what have I done? How was I to know you thought——'

'Oh, don't give me that,' he said savagely. 'I'm not entirely stupid—though very nearly. Of *course* you knew I didn't know your marriage had never been consummated. You didn't have the decency to tell me. You just didn't care! It's about time I realized what you're really like. You must have known—the other night up the Rock of Ages—what I thought. Of course you did—don't bother to lie. It sort of protected you, didn't it? When I think of it I realize what a colossal sort of fool I am. I tried to put myself in your place ... I thought Godfrey had made marriage so perfect for you, you wouldn't risk another marriage——

'I'm not a patient man by any means, by nature, or by discipline, yet I was prepared to school myself to wait till you were ready to relinquish the past and take life on again. But it wasn't that at all. You're merely clinging to the memory of a ceremony at a bedside and you're too damned selfish to enter fully into life again. So you let me make a fool of myself in front of everyone tonight. Perhaps it's the sort of thing I ought not to say, but I'll say it and be damned to you ... I don't think Godfrey would have approved all this *and* that you ought to have entered a nunnery! Oh, go inside!'

Henrietta fled, but when she got to the porch door, she paused, her cloak held round her, shivering though the night was warm and balmy. Because Charles was at the phone just inside the work kitchen and he'd wonder why on earth they were coming in separately. She'd wait till he finished talking.

Presently Johnny loomed out of the darkness. She turned round and said in a low voice, 'I'm just waiting till Charles is finished talking. I thought they'd think it odd if we came in separately.'

'Well, they ought to be getting used to odd behaviour. Oh, come on then, we'll go in together.'

As they came into the kitchen Charles said, looking up, 'Oh, here he is now. Just a moment, Deirdre.'

Deirdre!

As she walked through the big kitchen Henrietta heard Johnny say, 'Oh, sure I know it, Deirdre. Not the exact postal address, mind you, but it's very near the New Zealand High Commissioner's residence. You could send it care of him. His staff would see it got to him.'

It sounded a trivial excuse for an expensive call. Was it Rodney's address she was after? Why? Would a wife lose a husband's address? Sounded phoney. Merely an excuse to ring Dragonshill and talk to Johnny. When Charles had answered, she must have concocted this.

Henrietta would have loved to have heard the subsequent conversation but could think of no excuse to wait around. She slipped her cloak off and went into Madame's room. Penny, on a cushion on the floor, said, 'Have some coffee, Henrietta, Charles has just made some. I didn't realize you'd be back so soon. Charles, pour out another cup, would you?'

Henrietta said, 'Oh, the visibility wasn't so good tonight, so we didn't stay. Thanks, Charles.'

She saw Charles give a startled look at the far window, where stars were clearly visible, and felt her face grow hot. But Penny said very quickly, 'Who was the call from, Charles?'

'That last one? From Deirdre, of all people. She wanted an address in Singapore from Johnny. Someone she wants Rodney to contact. But, blast it, she wants to know if she can come here for a week before the bridge function. It seems she can get a ride with someone as far as Tekapo. Someone from here will have to get her. Perhaps Mike would do it for us if we're flat out.'

Penny said, 'Oh, dear, I can think of lots of people I'd rather have here at that busiest of all times than Deirdre. Anyway, she's a first-rate driver, so what's wrong with driving herself down, just the day before? Or does she think our garages on the river-bank aren't good enough to house her kind of car? It will be just one degree less plutey than a Rolls, I guess!'

Madame coughed. 'I think I may have been responsible for this, *chérie*, so please forgive. When I rang Deirdre she said she'd not been at all well and she'd be very pleased to come as she thought the mountain air would pick her up. I thought it a long way to come for so short a time and said if she wanted to come a few days beforehand, I was sure she would be welcome. But now I have made for you a little difficulty, *hein*?'

Penny softened immediately. 'No, no, Grand'mère ... sorry if I sounded prickly, but I think that for Johnny s sake I'll ask Hilary if she'll put Deirdre up.'

Henrietta said calmly, 'I don't think you need worry about Johnny's feelings at all, Penny.'

Madame permitted herself a little smile. 'Indeed no. Deirdre has quite lost her power to charm him. Had I known that, I should never have asked her here. But I think Henrietta once made a great bogey out of Johnny's brief and foolish infatuation, and when I knew they would be here together—Johnny and Henrietta—I thought if once she saw Johnny and Deirdre together, that bogey would be exorcised for ever. But from what I saw later in that so unromantic place, the store-room, I did not need to contrive.' The old black eyes twinkled naughtily.

Henrietta drew in a deep breath and tried desperately to think what to say. At that moment Johnny came into the room. Charles looked up.

'Johnny, there was another call just before that one, also from Christchurch. They wanted you at the Lands and Survey Department there. No, no hitch about the bridge. Merely that they want your advice on the further development of this area. You'll have time to get up and back before Christmas. We'll look after things this end. The men will be packing it in the day before Christmas Eve, anyway.'

But Johnny didn't come back for Christmas. He sent them a telegram that the Post Office rang through to them, to say he was spending Christmas in Christchurch.

CHAPTER SEVEN

THERE was none so gay at Dragonshill that Christmas as Henrietta King. The children found her great fun. She entered into every rustling secret for the Christmas tree, was tireless at pinning up decorations, hummed gay little tunes as she perched on step-ladders and tables, went for long forays into the rather distant pockets of bush for sprays of red *rata* and the equally red native mistletoe, loops of supplejack that were so excellent for twining coloured paper round, and clumps of native ferns in pots for all the corners.

But when someone proposed going to Evergreen Valley for some special ferns that grew there, she demurred. No, she wanted nothing to remind her of an idyll that had lasted less than a day.

The Dragonshill garden bloomed as it had never bloomed before. It was always a short season here and autumn flowers like chrysanthemums were out of the question, but Penny and Charles had forced the summer flowers to bloom early and richly by bringing in vast quantities of rich bush compost and manure.

The roses rioted over all the fences, purple and pink and lilac clematis garlanded the arches, every rock crevice sprang frothy alyssum, nasturtiums and livingstone daisies and portulaca carpeted the shingly soil with living patchwork and madonna lilies looked as if they had been carved out of ivory, they were so perfect. Perhaps it was because they had so long a season here without flowers that every plant was named and precious.

'Though even when every stalk is blackened and hideous, or buried under a foot of snow,' said Penny, gathering sweet peas, 'I know it's only a resting-time for the flowers, and I think of my garden as just lying fallow, never dead.' She turned impulsively to Henrietta. 'And life's like that at times too, Henrietta. Queenie said that once.'

When Henrietta didn't reply, she added purposely, 'She said it of you ... that your feelings were lying fallow, and that the second blooming might be the best of all for you. Queenie's a wonderful person, Henrietta, she'd never want you to be tied for always to Godfrey's memory.'

Henrietta, her arms full of white gypsophila, and her face above it as white as the flowers, said, 'I know Queenie wouldn't expect it, but it isn't as simple as all that. You mean Johnny, of course. But there are things between us that have nothing whatever to do with Godfrey.'

Penny wasn't one to be deterred. 'Then it's true what Grand'mère said ... that you've made a bogey out of Deirdre. Oh, Henrietta, we don't all marry our first loves. I mean I certainly didn't. Charles did. I was the only girl he ever loved.' She giggled, 'That is, as far as I know! But I was absolutely swept off my feet, before I met Charles, by a chap called Dennis, a male counterpart of Deirdre—selfish to the core. I realized it in time and broke it off. Then I met Charles and what I had felt for Dennis was nothing to what I felt for him. But my former engagement snarled things up for us, somewhat, just the same.' She giggled again, because Henrietta needed desperately, she was sure, to see the funny side of things. 'And the most awful thing happened. Just as things were coming right, Dennis turned up here. No idea I was here, of course. You know that Cabinet Minister—now retired—who is coming to the ceremony, Mr. Dreaverhill? Well, he's coming because of a long-ago incident here, when he and an official party got stranded. And, heaven help me, Dennis was with them. It was awful. Dennis had no sense of humour. And he sat on some royal blue Plasticine! But even if I hadn't broken it off, seeing him and Charles together would have convinced me it had been nothing but infatuation. You know, when the true gods come, the lesser gods go. And that's all it was with Johnny and Deirdre. He had a lucky escape.'

Henrietta said quietly, 'Ah, but that was a little different. You gave Dennis up. It was Deirdre who ditched Johnny. And it upset him so much he took off for the wilds.'

'Yes, but it's as dead as a *huia* now. And it was still the luckiest thing that ever happened to him. Imagine having anyone as cloying as Deirdre hanging round your neck for the rest of your life! Anyway, she married someone else, and if you can see Johnny as the type to let himself even long after someone else's wife, I can't! So don't be daft.'

But did any of them really know Johnny? Johnny who could whistle down the wind just as blithely when he was homesick as when he was happy. Johnny who whistled to keep his courage up. Johnny who even now was in Christchurch with Deirdre ...

Well, if John Carruthers could whistle to keep his courage up so could Henrietta King. She had a future here, with the children of the high country. It would take a great load off the minds of the Dragonshill women to know their children were being taught by a fully qualified teacher and she loved them all dearly.

No more lonely flats with only Godfrey's picture on her mantel and a prosaic proposal tucked away, with a sentimental poem that didn't mean a thing. Here you got to grips with life, felt needed and appreciated. Perhaps some day she would look back on these foolish longings and unfulfilled desires and laugh at herself.

Older people were always saying 'This too will pass.' Some day it would be true for her, too. Only it had been a long time passing.

Meanwhile Henrietta would enjoy herself. Why wilt at home when Johnny was in Christchurch, probably kidding himself Deirdre needed a male escort with her husband in Singapore? Very, very odd for a man to be away from his wife at Christmas ... air travel was so easy these days and money was no deterrent to Rodney Santos.

Charles said suddenly, 'Johnny will be back on New Year's Eve. It's fantastic, you know. We're bang in the middle of the summer holidays, yet the men are coming back to work. Either Johnny's personality is very persuasive, or the men have fallen under Grand'mère's spell—a bit of both, I'd think—because with the exception of two men whose arrangements for the holidays had been made too far ahead to change, the whole lot of them are taking their holidays later in the year and they'll all turn up here after New Year's Day. They want to have the approach this side as near finished as possible for the big day. Though even if they hadn't, we could have managed. I mean the foundation plaque could have been unveiled just the same. But Johnny's a grand chap. He wants it to look as near finished as can be so that Grand'mère can have a very clear picture in her mind of what it will be like when completed. I wish Johnny had known Grandpère. They are—would have been, I mean—two of a kind. How hard it is, when people one loves dies, to speak of them in the past tense. So Johnny will be coming back on New Year's Eve.'

'Did he ring you from Christchurch?' asked Penny, rather shortly.

'Yes. This morning. But Walter and Arene wanted me back in the pens immediately after. I took the call at the shed.'

Penny said, 'I wish he'd spoken to me—but I remember I'd switched the phone down there. I'd have got him to bring me some stuff from Christchurch. I was thinking of ringing him at his hotel this afternoon.'

'Well, you'd better make it first thing tomorrow morning when you'll be bound to catch him. He was spending the day with friends at Bryndwyr and they were just going off to the power-station at Lake Coleridge, he said.'

Bryndwyr. Deirdre Santos lived in Bryndwyr. Henrietta felt slightly sick.

Walter looked up from his apple pie. 'Henrietta, be my partner at the New Year's Eve Ball in Tekapo? Johnny may not get back till late, or I'd not dare ask, but I'd love to take you.'

Henrietta said warmly, 'And I'd love to go with you, Walter. You're about the best dancer I know. And Johnny's never said he wanted to go. There's no ball like the New Year's Eve one. I take it that it's still a Hogmanay Ball, with quite a few kilts and the women wearing sashes of tartan?'

'Yes. We have a supply of sashes for those who haven't got them. But perhaps Queenie will have one for you?'

'M'm. She keeps a lot in her old tin trunk. Mine is a Gunn tartan, of course.'

Oh, yes. There was plenty of gaiety to keep Henrietta from dwelling on thoughts of Johnny. What matter if everyone had found a present from him at the foot of the Christmas tree except Henrietta. It went unnoticed, she thought, in the multitude of parcels and the crowd of the two families, because everyone from Two Thumbs homestead was present too.

Only Queenie asked, when she and Mike arrived for Christmas tea. Fortunately no one else was near enough to hear. Henrietta had gone over in the truck with Walter, to pick them up from the far bank, and he and Mike were so busy talking sheep they did not hear Queenie's question.

Henrietta pretended to consider it. 'There were so many presents,' she said. 'Let me see . . . no, there wasn't one, unless that Agatha Christie was from him. No, I'm pretty sure Pierre gave me that.'

Queenie said comfortably, 'He'll be bringing you something special from Christchurch.'

Henrietta said, 'If he thinks of it. But I'm afraid I've nothing for him. We've not even exchanged cards for years.'

No, but a present bought weeks ago for him lay at

the bottom of her wardrobe. A beautifully bound book of poetry.

Hilary set everybody's hair beautifully for the Ball, piling Henrietta's into layered whorls. Walter, surveying it, whistled.

'My partner will knock 'em all cold,' he vowed. 'Gosh, Hilary, it's a good job you didn't make it an inch higher, or she'd top me. I'm not as tall as Johnny, you know.'

'Aren't you?' asked Henrietta carelessly. 'I'd have thought you were. But he's broader, so it brings his height down. But you're a much better dancer than he is, Walter.'

They all dressed at Kings' because long frocks and the back of a four-wheel-drive truck swishing through river-streams didn't exactly go together.

Johnny hadn't arrived at the homestead. He must be coming back the day the men were—after New Year. Queenie started to say something, checked herself and said, 'Henrietta, I've never seen you in red before. What a glorious shade, and with that green Gunn tartan sash it's just perfect.'

Henrietta flushed a little, said, 'And Penny made me wear her emerald necklace and earrings. I'm terrified anything happens to them. I'd hate to lose a stone.'

She touched them caressingly. 'I feel I'm linked with history. These came out of France with Madame's grandparents at the time of the Revolution. It almost seems sacrilege for them to be worn at a backblocks dance at the bottom of the world.'

'Not if they're worn by someone who cares about history,' said a voice from the hall doorway. Johnny's voice.

Henrietta looked across the heads to see him standing there. Oh, damn, damn ... must she always feel like this? Would she never school this twenty-nine-year-old heart of hers to stop behaving like a moonstruck teenager's?

Then her heart steadied, slowed its racing, because just behind him was Deirdre. An older Deirdre certainly, but every bit as beautiful as ever and with a delicacy of feature and colouring that was essentially feminine and heart-stirring.

Queenie said, 'Oh, you made it after all. Are you feeling better, Deirdre?'

Deirdre nodded. 'Those friends of Johnny's in Fairlie were very good. I lay down for two hours.' She spread her hands out in a rueful gesture. 'So unromantic! I was car-sick. I thought I might have to spend the night, but it must have been just the heat of the day, because I feel much better—tired, with the long journey, but not squeamish any more despite the bends on Burke's Pass.'

Queenie said matter-of-factly, 'Deirdre is going to stay with me. I told Johnny when he rang that it would be less for Hilary to do, at such a busy time, and it will be good company for me.'

Queenie could always get away with such statements. Deirdre didn't look at all put out. Henrietta knew a wave of gratitude to Queenie wash over her. At least it would be better than having her on the station. The gratitude was succeeded by a most unworthy thought ... she just wished there'd be heavy rain in the back country. There wasn't enough snow left for a heavy thaw, but say an electrical storm, and, close to the watersheds of the Alps as they were, the river could be up in two hours. How lovely to have all the treacherousness of the Pawerawera between Johnny and Deirdre! What a ghastly thing to hope for! A flood now would put paid to getting the bridge approach finished for the big day.

Henrietta said now to Walter, 'I do want to be there for the start of the Ball. The Robertsons hate late starts, and it's such fun I don't want to miss a moment of it. It will probably take Deirdre a little while to change.' (Hours, probably, and Deirdre never one to worry that she was spoiling anyone else's night!)

As she passed by Johnny her eyes met his. 'See you later, then,' he said coolly, and Henrietta went past him in a faint aura of white rose perfume.

The Robertson homestead was the perfect setting for a ball, with lights through all the trees, and the ballroom, a relic of pioneer days, ablaze with lights from beginning to end, set on a rise above the garden. This could have been enchantment, thought Henrietta, poignancy squeezing her emotions. It had been the scene of her first grown-up dance, at seventeen, the dance she'd never forget because Johnny had been her partner and for the first time she'd felt not a schoolgirl, but a woman. And dancing in his arms she'd dreamed dreams.

He'd said, 'Why, Henrietta, you dance like a bit of thistledown. And in that dress I find it hard to remember what a holy terror you used to be.'

Nevertheless, with fiddles and accordions playing, and occasionally the pipes, it was impossible not to enjoy oneself, even if, over the shoulders of her partners, she kept watching the doors for the entrance of Deirdre and Johnny. But she didn't see them come in.

It was almost suppertime when he suddenly appeared among the crowd. Walter was escorting Henrietta back to their group and she was glowing with the sheer enjoyment of dancing with so perfect a partner. Johnny seemed to simply materialize.

She blinked. 'Where did you get your kilt from?'

He grinned. 'I left it at Queenie's all through the years. I could do no less than don it when she'd gone to all the trouble of pressing it, could I? But it's just as well that it's a short session for me tonight. As you might remember it belonged to Mother's father. That's why it's a Mackay tartan. And it so happens I take after Dad for build. Granddad was a very spare man. This is giving me a pain round my fifth rib. I didn't let on to Queenie. She was all for hustling me off here.'

Henrietta had a queer feeling. She was all confused. They had parted in terrible anger. Now he was back to their old footing ... brotherly. As they had been all those years ago. Would anyone ever understand Johnny?

Presently he said, 'Nothing to say to me, Henrietta? What's the matter?'

She turned a little way to isolate them from the others. She said sharply, 'Johnny, last time we met, I bore the brunt of your tongue. How can you expect me just to overlook that? I just don't understand your sudden rages—your equally sudden exalted moods—I don't think I can go along with them any longer. And I don't know where I am or what you're at. Nor does anyone else.'

'Wrong,' he said, just as the music started again, and he took hold of her and steered her into the dancers. 'Queenie knows very well what I'm at, she always knows, bless her. I'm a good deal happier now than when I went away.'

Happier now? Because Deirdre was here? Yet why should Henrietta find that hard to understand? Even if Deirdre was married to someone else, perhaps it was enough just to have her near. It could make this present time a little happier for him, she supposed. After all, Charles's head shepherd was twice the dancer Johnny was, but being in Walter's arms didn't mean a thing. Whereas being in Johnny's was ... heaven.

Johnny said, 'Yes, I bawled you out. And I had a right to, girl; sometimes I feel I just must try to shatter your complacency ... disturb that maddening self-sufficiency. Yet I always hate myself when I do it. I've an idea that loneliness still stalks you in your weaker hours.'

Dancing on, Henrietta said, 'I can do fine without your pity. And perhaps it's not so much complacency ... that smacks of smugness ... but it's contentment. So don't bother to disturb it. I enjoy life as I live it at the moment.'

The music ended and they found themselves beside old Mac Robertson. He surveyed them both. 'Good that you could both be here. Like old times.' He twinkled. 'Nice to see a Gunn and a Mackay at peace with each other. They were aye enemies, though they have been known to intermarry.'

'I think,' said Johnny solemnly, 'that marrying is more in my line than fighting. Mac, I think Bruce McNaught is after you.' He peered into Henrietta's face. 'I see the signs of temper. What are you mad about now?'

'You know very well,' said Henrietta shortly. 'Gunns and Mackays intermarrying! Oh, pah! You make me mad,' and she went swiftly across the room.

What was all this talk but throwing dust in the eyes? ... so no one should guess he still carried a torch for Deirdre Santos. Perhaps he thought this couple of weeks would be the last he would ever share with Deirdre. And after that he had a future, a future that when this bridge was finished, would carry him away from New Zealand to places where a wife could make all the difference to a man's comfort. He's decided to overlook the fact that I wasn't open with him about my marriage. Oh, no, John Carruthers, I will *not* be used like that!

She did not dance with him again, although he asked her. She had plenty of excuses and played the part of one who was enjoying herself to the hilt. Penny, watching her closely, thought she was almost fey tonight. And certainly she had never looked more beautiful, with that lovely flush high on her cheekbones and the lights from the chandeliers making golden stars dance in her hair and in her peat-brown eyes. The swinging emeralds, pendant from her ears, the green of her sash across the scarlet of her frock, the lilt in her voice and the carriage of her head, were all part of a mood of gaiety, almost abandon. Penny was fiercely glad Deirdre had not come, with her pale magic and her seemingly irresistible charm.

Henrietta, dancing with old Duncan Gray and giving him the thrill of his evening, heard Penny say to Charles with great satisfaction, 'Didn't you think Deirdre had put on a bit of weight, darling?'

She didn't hear the answer, but what did it matter? Not to Johnny, who openly avowed he didn't care for skinny women. She supposed even Uncle Mike had succumbed to her charm since he had elected to stay with Deirdre and had sent Queenie along with Johnny.

It was three in the morning before they reached Pukewhetu with everyone still in high spirits and ready to help Queenie cook them bacon-and-eggs and to sit round the huge kitchen table to eat it, after Henrietta, because she was dark, had first-footed Uncle Mike.

Deirdre in a turquoise quilted gown over a filmy nightgown, drifted out, yawning and rubbing her eyes and looking delectable enough to eat. But she shuddered delicately at the thought of such hearty food at this ungodly hour of the morning and subsided into the big chair by the old coal range. Henrietta noted ironically that even if she was pretending she had just wakened up, not a hair was out of place, and either she'd not washed her make-up off when she went to bed, or had renewed it at the sounds of their arrival. Also that the chair she had selected was the nearest one to Johnny's. But who cared?

'Feeling better now?' asked Johnny gently.

'Yes, much. I honestly don't know how you high country folk stand up to all this. It's a far more hectic pace than in the cities. And you've still got to go umpteen miles and ford that horrible river.'

'Well, Henrietta seems able to take it in her stride again, and doesn't seem to be sighing for that easier, glittering diplomatic world. But we have to put on a show like this once in a while in case she hungers for the flesh-pots.'

Deirdre smiled, 'I've no doubt she finds compensa-

144

tions,' and looked knowing.

Johnny laughed. 'Yes, I heard her saying she'd not met a better dancer than Walter in either London or New York.'

Henrietta saw Penny's brows come down in a scowl and wanted to laugh. Deirdre hadn't changed much. She wasn't interested in Walter, but she'd hint that Henrietta was. Well, who cared? She certainly didn't, and if Johnny couldn't see through Deirdre after the way she'd dumped him when a wealthier chap came on her horizon, he deserved to burn his fingers again at that particular fire. Thinking this made Henrietta feel much better.

They left their finery in Queenie's wardrobes and, equipped for the river crossing in trews and turtle-necked sweaters, piled into the cars and went up the lakeside road to the river-truck. No one cared what time they got home since Arene and his wife and children were spending the night at the homestead with the little ones and Madame.

Squashed into the back of the truck, with Charles driving and Penny and Hilary beside him, under cover of some spirited teasing Judy and Brigid were having with the shepherds who had partnered them, Johnny said in Henrietta's ear, 'I've decided to bury our particular hatchet till the bridge ceremony is over. This fortnight is going to be packed with work for a start, and if there is one thing that is more important than anything else, it is that nothing must even slightly ruffle Madame's happiness at this time.'

Henrietta said in a whisper, 'How extremely comforting to know that. I'd just like to point out that I wasn't the one who lost my temper—even though you doubted my word, which was most provoking—*you* were the one who blew your top and bawled me out. I'm all in favour of a quiet life. It's what I came up here for. I thought it was going to be an ideal existence ... the high country I love so well, the children and the chance of teaching again. That's my life. It's what I trained for. So you needn't worry about hatchets. I just want tranquillity from now on.'

'Sounds a bit dull to me,' said John Carruthers.

But it was a schooled tranquillity. Henrietta was conscious of pain beneath the surface whenever she saw Johnny taking the truck at nights when the long, heavy day's work was through and fording the river to go down the rough miles to Pukewhetu.

Let's face it, Henrietta, she told herself sternly, he didn't go as often as this to see Mike about those culverts before Deirdre came.

She heard Penny say to Charles once, 'What's he going off to Pukewhetu so much for? Doug said to me on the phone yesterday that the last of the culverts for the track to his new house were finished three days ago.'

Charles answered, 'Oh, he aye went to Queenie when he wanted a bit of comfort. He looks like a self-sufficient joker, but he isn't. He never was. He was a lonely little tyke, you know, with his parents always away.'

Henrietta put herself out of range of their voices and busied herself with some energetic weeding. She didn't want to remember the lonely little tyke who'd understood so well her own loneliness. Much better to think of him as the arrogant bridge-builder who thought he could get whatever he wanted.

Twice before the day of the ceremony he actually took time off to fetch Deirdre to Dragonshill for the day. Certainly he brought Queenie too, but it was Deirdre he took to the approach site. He was even quite tolerant of her fear of the big machinery, her obvious lack of rapport with the tough, good-hearted labourers.

He brought her back to the homestead for afternoon tea and stayed to have some with them. Usually he could hardly bear to take time off the location.

Deirdre said, 'Did you say this was child's play compared to some of your overseas jobs? Then I'd hate to think what they must be like.'

Johnny laughed, his mouth full of buttered scone. He finished it, said, 'There's everything in our favour here ... good, solid rock, firm foundations, a few hazards later no doubt, with floodwaters from rain and thaw, but nothing like some of the South American jobs. Mosquitoes and a thousand other biting, stinging things, scorpions, snakes, bog, alligators, evil-smelling swamps, often trouble among the men. Sometimes you run up against a real snag in the matter of language, though I'm making out with that now. The feeling of oppression the jungle gives you. It's so prolific, so ready to spring back and encroach again, to trap you. And sometimes the threat of hostile tribes.'

Deirdre shuddered. 'I don't know how you take it. It's even worse than what Madame had to face up to here in the early years.'

Madame said, but gently, 'I did it because I loved François. And for my François there just had to be this battling with the elements, this wresting of a living from a harsh, uninhabited world. And for me, he made it all worth while. Never, never did François forget the little refinements. Some men can become hardened by their environment, you understand? And for their women it becomes a grievance. But my husband knew so well the little things that count. Other women, in circumstances like these, would, I am sure, have had things practical for their birthdays, their wedding anniversaries. Like an extra colonial oven, or an iron kettle, but François, he always made it jewellery, or flowers. Only twice was he ever able to bring me flowers from a florist, you understand, but he would be away for hours in the bush to find the little wild orchids, or the mountain lilies.

'Nothing could be more beautiful than the mountain lilies. So purely white, with their orange stamens, and their great saucer-like leaves, each with a drop of dew in them. I said once I wondered why they were called lilies, when they were really ranunculi, and François, who was like you, Johnny in that he knew so many things and remembered them, said that when Christ talked of the lilies of the field, He meant the little wild anemones and ranunculi that carpeted the pastures there.'

She was silent for a moment, dreaming of the past, a little smile playing about her lips. Then she said, 'I longed for roses to grow here. François built me a little shelter fence of scrub, and brought me soil from the forest floor, then he took a trip to town. Those were the days when the stores came in only once a year, with the wagons that came through the river to take our wool-clip out, but just sometimes a special trip had to be made. He went to Timaru this time, buying in sheep and doing much business. It took days, of course. I could not go, would not risk it because I was expecting again and this time, at last, I wished to carry my child full time. I did. It was Carl and Francis's mother, my Marguerite.

'All day I had scanned the river-bed for a glimpse of François, from the lookout. There was a slight fresh in the river, but not a lot of water. But it looked like rain to me and I did not want it to rise and maroon François on the opposite bank as it had once, for two whole weeks. I prayed he might get here before the light faded.

'He did, and came through with the dray. I was down on the shingle, watching. In the last stream of all suddenly the water scoured out under the offside wheel and part of the load went over. But it righted itself and to my horror I saw François plunge in and swim after one bit of merchandise tied up in sacking.

'I ran up and down, calling to him to let it go, but he got it and struggled out much further down where the current had carried him. The horse dragged the dray out and when François got to me I lost my temper. *Ma foi*, how I stormed at him! I said did he not care that I, a woman with child, might have been left alone in the mountains, that I had no patience with foolhardiness, that men were cruel to their wives in their disregard of danger ... oh, how I railed! I said a dozen things I hated to recall ever afterwards.

'And when I stopped because I was out of breath, François just smiled and held out the sodden bundle of sacking and said, "But they were your roses, *mignonne*, I could not let *them* go." and I sat down and cried.' Madame Beaudonais pointed to the trellis outside. 'And they still bloom every year, tended and cherished by my grandsons. Those creamy clusters and that deep red one. We never knew their names, because the writing was washed off the labels.'

Penny and Henrietta had to blink rapidly to clear their eyes of unshed tears then they stared. Deirdre was unashamedly wiping her tears away. Deirdre! She said, 'Madame, I can't think how you bore it ... the isolation, the loss of your babies ... but I envy you your courage, your fortitude ... a lesser woman would have taken your François from his beloved mountains.'

Johnny got up to go back to work. He passed Deirdre's chair, and quite openly patted her hand.

Once more Henrietta was conscious of a conflict of feelings. This Deirdre was different, but infinitely more dangerous! There was something to admire in her now, and a radiance about her that was very disturbing, as if some deep happiness shone out of her rather than upon her. Was it seeing Johnny again? What had he meant about no woman being worth very much till she had been through a great deal of sadness, of wanting what she could not get?

What did Deirdre want? Was it Johnny? Was the reason she could not get what she wanted, Rodney? And Rodney was staying away. Thinking things out?

Deirdre, according to Uncle Mike, was pulling her-weight at Pukewhetu. He was full of praise for her. 'I used to think she was just a lily of the field, but she both toils and spins now. And Johnny tells me she's a simply wonderful housekeeper. He visited her in Christchurch, you know. Perhaps she found her right sphere. Rodney needs a hostess for all his business entertaining. It seems she does it right royally. I expect it was just that as a child she needed more bottom-smacking. She was hopelessly spoiled. These children are more to be pitied than blamed. And some, like Deirdre, turn out all right after all.' He had grinned. 'Love's a wonderful thing. Can change people overnight. I've got to hand it to you women, you are incredibly adaptable. Always following your men.'

But Deirdre hadn't followed her man. She hadn't followed the dictates of her heart. She'd very conveniently found a man whose way of life had suited her, and nevertheless couldn't stop herself from looking back longingly over her shoulder to the man she had truly loved.

Yes, Deirdre had worked her usual spell upon the menfolk. But not upon Queenie. She came to Dragonshill one night with Johnny.

This was quite surprising as Queenie was one who just hated spending a night away from her own bed and hearthside.

'Oh,' she said, 'I just wanted a bit crack with Madame before all the fuss and flummery of the big day descends upon us. And Deirdre can look after Mike. It's not every day I've the chance of having a good cook in the house. In that, at least, she's changed for the better.

'I said at the time that Rodney Santos was the man for her. He wouldn't stand for any nonsense. He saw through every one of her tricks and poses. He loved her in spite of them but wouldn't let her get away with any. He still won't. He makes her toe the line all right. I thought he would, with a chin like that.'

But next morning Henrietta found out the real reason for Queenie's visit. She heard Penny say, 'I'll take Grand'mère and the children over to Two

Thumbs, and you can wangle your warning to Henrietta.'

Wangle! Warning!

If it hadn't mattered so much to Henrietta, she'd have been chuckling inwardly at the trouble Queenie went to in her endeavours to make the conversation appear the natural outcome of casual talk.

Perversely Henrietta headed her off twice, then Queenie got round to it by reminiscing about the old days. 'They were so idyllic, with none of us ever dreaming of what lay ahead.'

That took Henrietta momentarily off guard. She put out a hand to one of Queenie's, touched it briefly, said, 'I know, Queenie. Because Godfrey seemed just brimming over with health. No one could have guessed.'

Queenie shook her head. 'I didn't mean that Henrietta. I thought I'd never get over that loss. But I've learned to live with it. I can think back now to the childhood memories without that dreadful stab of being unable to believe he wasn't still living. And I often dream about him, happy dreams. But I meant Johnny. What happened to *him*.'

Henrietta didn't follow it up, but Queenie went on, 'When you're young disillusionment is hard to bear, and—like you—he has known much loneliness in his life. I felt when he was young, as I did with you, that I'd like life to make that up to him. I did grieve for him when Deirdre jilted him, though I thought he'd had a lucky escape as she was then. But life has a habit of presenting us with second chances. Don't let your pride, your very natural pride, stand in your way now. Pride is a cold companion.'

Henrietta said, rather drearily, 'It's not just pride, Queenie. There are other things. It's a big step linking your life to someone and not knowing if it's the right thing to do.'

Queenie struck her hands together impatiently. 'If only you were sweet-and-twenty again you'd not hesitate. It's being twenty-nine that does it. You're weighing up the risks too much. I'd stake anything that you and Johnny would make a go of it. Henrietta, perhaps you're looking for perfection. You know marriage has to be worked at. I well remember the week before I married Mike, wondering if I was taking the right step. I was so idealistic I didn't think I'd have it in me to carry on if things didn't just go my way. But I found out Mike's faults and he found out mine, and although we didn't start that way, we became two of a kind.'

She didn't convince Henrietta. She tried one more tack before she left. 'You ought to think more of Johnny than of yourself. If ever a man needs you, Johnny does.'

Henrietta's tone was tinged with bitterness. 'Every-one thinks that. That I can take his sort of life.'

'That wasn't what I had in mind. Johnny's in danger. Deirdre is twice as fascinating as she was before. He saw through her before, saw the shallowness, the calculating mind of her, when she took Rodney who was established in life and established well. But now there's more to her—oh, Henrietta!'

And she left the rest to Henrietta's already over-worked imagination.

It was all very painful because so much else was ideal ...

Henrietta would never forget the sheer perfection of the special thanksgiving service at the Church of the Good Shepherd at Tekapo, when all the Mackenzie Country turned out to pay their tribute to this gallant woman who could remember back to the early days of this Alpine district; who had gone so far into the mountains, she had been beyond the end of the road that led west.

There was the simplicity and yet grandeur of that bare hillside where the little stone church stood, sturdy as the lake-boulders that formed it. The sun shone blindingly on the golden tussocks of the bare hillside above the lake, and inside the church the altar window with its cross silhouetted against the scene, framed the turquoise blue of the lake and the shining peaks of the mountains.

The small church could not accommodate all who came, but they had amplifiers outside and the people crowded about the windows and spread down the hillside, and tourists passing, paused in amazement, whispered questions and came to join in the thanksgiving and to sing with them.

Madame was very erect, and looked inspired rather than weary, and it was a day no one would ever forget, the crown of a century of living.

CHAPTER EIGHT

It was just three days to the ceremony when Deirdre spent a whole day at Dragonshill. Queenie had come over with her, bringing a huge lot of goodies for the banquet, but Francis had taken her back over the river by lunch-time. Johnny had asked Deirdre to stay on, had said it in front of all of them.

'But you don't have to go back now, do you, Deirdre?'

Even Deirdre had looked a little surprised. 'Well, we can't just come and go here as we please, John, can we?'

He'd said, grinning, 'It's only when it's in flood that we allow that river to interfere with our pleasures. Can't let it become top-dog, you know. I'll run you back before dusk.'

Deirdre said, 'I'll only stay if I'm allowed to help. If I'm going to be treated as a visitor, I won't.'

Even Penny thawed at this, but Johnny was foolish, just the same, to want to burn his fingers twice. Penny said crisply, 'Right, I'll take you up on that. We certainly can't entertain anyone. If you like to clean the silver, I'd be very happy. I've more than enough to do without that, and it's far too big a job for Henrietta on her own. Now, off with you, Johnny. This is no place this morning for non-combatants. We want no distractions.'

There, thought Penny. Silver-cleaning is a hateful job, and if she doesn't want to soil her fingers, she can go with Queenie. Henrietta thought desperately: 'He just can't help loving her any more than I can help loving him. He wants her here all day when he'll be at the river all the time, just for the sheer joy of driving her home in the mountain dusk. But where will that

154

get him?'

Deirdre proved knacky with flowers too, and that freed the rest of them to making up spare beds and taking piles of linen down to the cottages where extra bunks had been put up. The workmen for this side were occupying the shearers' quarters and their own huts. 'Thank heaven they have such a good cook,' said Penny. 'Some of the ones who come with the shearers are the limit. Either they seem to be good cooks but hardly ever sober, or sober and no more capable of serving an appetizing meal than a giraffe would be. I'm sure I don't know why. Some are gentle souls, too much so for the tough ones, and others are men who've become so tough themselves that they can't open their mouths without swearing. But this one is a gem. They all like him. He's a splendid influence.'

After dinner Penny flopped and said, 'Well, we've broken the back of it. Nobody is going to expect absolute perfection when we're catering for such a crowd, and the Guild at Tekapo is going to do all the serving on the day itself, so I think that the next two days we should not overdo, or we won't be fit to enjoy the big day itself. And until that plaque is cemented into place, I shan't really be able to believe that someday we'll have a bridge, that that river will no longer bully us and dictate our comings and goings.'

She added, 'Best of all, I'll be able to keep governesses. Once they know they can go home for weekends *when they like* there won't be half the trouble.'

Henrietta looked amazed. Then she laughed. 'That's looking ahead with a vengeance, isn't it? I thought I'd been offered a permanent position.' She grinned. 'Perhaps the greatest of all conveniences will be that you'll even be able to sack a governess occasionally instead of going down on your knees to get one.'

Deirdre tucked back a straying pale gold tendril of hair into her roll and said, 'I should imagine Penny means when you marry again, Henrietta. I can't see you staying a widow for ever.'

It was said very nicely. Henrietta merely shrugged.

Johnny looked out of the window. 'I think we'd better move, Deirdre.' He looked across at Charles. 'Will you put the guide lights on for me, in case it's dark when I get back?'

'I will. What time?'

'Oh, any time from nine to eleven, I suppose. I want to see Queenie.'

See Queenie! Oh, be honest with yourself, Johnny Carruthers ... you want to show Deirdre Lake Tekapo in all its sunset beauty ... and to linger ...

They had been gone just a few moments when Penny said, 'Oh, Deirdre has forgotten her bag. Henrietta, fly after them, will you? They'll not have got the truck out of the shed yet.'

Henrietta picked it up and ran, her jandals making no sound as she sped across the soft dust of the yard. They were standing by the side of the truck, talking seriously. Their tones stopped Henrietta in her tracks.

Then she heard Deirdre say, in a low intense tone, 'It's just not working, you know, Johnny. I never did think it would work. And it makes me feel so unnatural, so artificial, so insincere.'

Johnny said soothingly, 'No need for you to feel like that. You're doing extremely well. No one will ever guess. After all, you said you owed it to me.'

'Yes, I do. No one knows that better than I. Oh, I hate myself for what I did all those years ago. Things could have been so different. If only I'd known how things would go ... but I was so selfish, thinking only of myself. But I've learned a lot since I married Rodney. I've got my values straight. Only you can't undo what you've already done.'

Henrietta had heard enough, more than enough. As silently as she had come, she retreated. Then at a safe distance she called out, 'Johnny ... Deirdre ... are you there?'

They came out. Henrietta was proud of her natural tone. 'Oh, thank goodness! Deirdre left her bag. We thought she might want it.'

'Oh, I do. Rodney's latest letter is there. It came just before we left this morning. I've only skimmed through it.'

Pretending to the last, thought Henrietta. And all the time egging Johnny on in private. She looked at him and an immense pity smote her. How odd ... she ought to be feeling angry with him. But it seemed to her as if Deirdre was only using him. Using him to end a marriage she was tired of? There could be some other man in her sights, someone whose name must not be sullied. Deirdre hadn't changed. She would never, never take Johnny's sort of life. But she might use him to get her freedom.

There was very little time to think about it. It just lay, a dead weight, on her spirits, while she pretended to enter into every moment of the joyous time ahead.

Nevertheless, by the eve of the big day Henrietta could think of nothing else but the significance of the occasion, this opening up of the high country, this end to remoteness, the wonder of knowing that in a few short months when that shining arch should span the River of Dread, no one here would know any more the agonizing helplessness of being cut off by a flooded river from medical aid when a man was injured, a child desperately ill, or a woman about to give premature birth.

By now the Two Thumbs homestead and Dragonshill itself were full to overflowing. The workmen on the site were back across the river staying in their Ministry of Works huts or in the shearers' quarters of the Llewellyns' estate, to leave all accommodation this side free for the guests.

There were Beaudonais relations from the little French settlement of Akaroa near Christchurch, where François Beaudonais had been born and whence he had gone to seek out the descendants of friends of his ancestors who had fled to England during the Revolution; Helmut and Franz Schmidt, German cousins of Charles and Francis, whose father had been a Schmidt, had chosen this year to visit New Zealand so they could share in this milestone, returning a visit Charles and Penny had made to Germany when they were first married, and were great favourites with all the children. A great-granddaughter of the first woman ever to live on Dragonshill, wife of a shepherd who had managed the run for an absentee owner, had flown down from Auckland; a great percentage of the shepherds who had worked on Dragonshill, plus many who had sheared there year after year, had come, and the governesses, especially important among them, Miss Tillyman, whose place Penny had taken a few years go.

Then of course there was the official part ... the Minister of Works, the Minister of Agriculture, the retired Minister of the Cabinet, who had been marooned there eight years ago, Mr. Dreaverhill.

He was Madame's special favourite. He had bowed low over her hand, kissed it, said, 'Madame, I thought you an impossibly young ninety-two when first I met you, but now I am astounded. No wonder your young ones love you dearly.'

'*Ma foi*,' said Madame, sparkling, 'but that is a very pretty speech, and I am a foolish old woman because I so like to hear you say it.'

Hilary had excelled herself with Madame's hair. The snowy tresses were piled high in shining overlaps, but tiny curls clustered round the broad, peaceful brow, softening the severity of the style. A sparkling ruby-and-diamond pin nestled among them, and she was wearing a ruby-coloured dress of some synthetic material that had all the elegance and richness of an old-world brocade, and it made her very much the *grande dame*. She had a velvet ribbon about her throat with a diamond pin and more diamonds flashed from her crêpey white fingers.

Hilary had added a touch of rouge to the high cheekbones and a soft pink lipstick and her incredibly dark eyes glowed with happiness.

'Is there any beauty like the beauty of an aged face?' said Johnny in Henrietta's ear. 'I mean the aged face that belongs to a woman who has lived richly and deeply as has Madame.'

She turned to meet his eyes over her shoulder. 'No,' she said, her voice shaking a little.

He continued, 'And look at Charlotte. Can't you imagine her, grown old, and looking just like Madame? I took a flashlight of the two of them a few moments ago, in Charles's study, with the background of that wall that's covered with mountain pictures, and the stack of skis in the corner. I'm so glad she has Madame's full name ... Charlotte Gregoire Beaudonais-Smith. It's so fitting.'

Dinner was over, the ceremonious dinner that Penny and Hilary had lovingly prepared, with Grand'mère at the head of her table, love beaming from her eyes, pride in the culinary achievements of her two grand-daughters-in-law shining out of her, the conversation of her distinguished guests evoking her still-dry wit, her ready laughter.

Enmity forgotten, Henrietta said to Johnny, 'She's almost fey tonight, as if she's existing on spirit alone. Oh, I do so hope she lasts to see your bridge finished, to actually walk across it and know that Dragonshill is linked with the rest of the world.'

They could have been in a world of their own, sharing a conversation as uninhibited as their long, idealistic discussions of long ago.

Johnny nodded, 'I've often thought that had this bridge not been started, Madame would have relinquished life as soon as her hundredth birthday was over. She said to me on that day as she read her congratulatory cable from the Queen, "This sets a seal on a very long life. I've lived on borrowed time many a year, Johnny, but I wouldn't forgo a moment of it. But all I ask now is that I am allowed to slip away, here at Dragonshill, without causing them too much bother." '

Henrietta was startled. She said in a low voice, 'I hadn't realized you were here for the birthday. It was the most bitter disappointment to me when I couldn't come. I'd taken my holidays then on purpose, but Rhona was taken ill suddenly—Jock's wife—and was rushed to hospital. She has no relatives in New Zealand at all, and the children were used to me. I just couldn't have left them. But nobody said you were here.'

'Of course not. Remember I'd told them—asked them—not to tell you.'

'I still can't figure why, Johnny. Either then, or on your later visit.'

His lips twisted. 'You ought to be able to figure it out. They told me you were coming back to be the governess here. I thought of your maddening elusiveness ... your *wounding* elusiveness, and said they'd probably lose a good governess if they told you that I was going to be here the best part of a year. Be honest, now, Henrietta, had you known I would be here, would you have come?'

The peaty-brown eyes flickered and fell before the steel-bright demanding eyes. A flush crept up her cheeks. Then she looked up and said frankly, 'Johnny ... I just don't know. Possibly.'

The buzz of conversation very effectively isolated them.

He said, with something in his tone she could not analyse, 'Well, that's something. For once you're answering me without trying to hide anything. Perhaps you're looking out of your ivory tower and admitting you'd like to return to ordinary living.'

Henrietta felt her lips go a little stiff. Oh, how she wished they were in a room by themselves!

She said, with difficulty, 'Would you—would you still want me to do just that, Johnny?'

She'd kept her eyes down this time so could not see his expression. But when he did answer, his voice was roughened. 'You didn't care enough, when you knew Deirdre was coming up here, even to want to protect

160

me a little, did you?'

Henrietta knew a sickening jolt.

She moistened her lips and said quite calmly, 'Protect you, Johnny? Since when have you seemed in need of protection?'

'You should know. I might seem self-sufficient to other people. But you *know* me. You're the only one, apart from Godfrey, ever to know how unbearably homesick I was for Mum and Dad ... so?'

She said very slowly, 'Protection from whom, Johnny? Not from Deirdre, surely? She has a husband.'

Her eyes were still cast down. But she could have sworn there was a smile in his voice. But why would that be? It was a very serious conversation.

He said, 'Did you never think I might need to be protected from myself?'

Her eyes flickered up then, uncertainty in them. 'Johnny, I just don't understand you. Isn't that an odd thing to say to a girl you——'

'A girl I once asked to marry me? Yes, it is. But then she's an extremely odd girl. It could be I'm trying to smoke her out of her ivory tower.'

She said swiftly, nervous lest anyone suddenly break in on them, 'What a time to start a conversation like this—we'll never sort it out now—but is it any wonder you have me so bewildered? I'll never forget how you reacted over the fact that—that all I ever had of Godfrey was his name. And about Deirdre ... what you said about protection. Is that likely to endear you to me? Oh, I just don't get it. Johnny——'

'Hold it! Charles is just coming in with the big old Family Bible. For the family devotions in preparation for the big day. Henrietta, it will have to wait. Wait till all the guests are gone and you and I are no longer at everyone's beck and call.'

He added, 'Madame has asked me to do the reading. I protested that one of her grandsons should do it, but she said that for one thing it meant discriminating between them and she loved them equally, but that for another, as I was building the bridge, I was to choose the reading and do it.'

Henrietta felt deeply moved. 'Johnny, I hope you've chosen something that will give tribute to yourself as well as to Madame. I mean—as far as your work is concerned, you are a modest man.'

He burst out laughing in the old guffawing way. 'Oh, Henrietta, you're priceless! You say that in the tone of one who gives the divil his due ... you're as good as saying that one of my few virtues is modesty ... and *that* only as far as my work is concerned!'

Henrietta's colour rose. 'If it sounded that way I didn't mean it. Only——'

'Only what? Don't spare me. You never do.'

'No, I won't finish it. I want harmony between us for this time that is meant to be happy. Did you have much trouble finding a reading? I suppose you'd want one with something about a bridge in it?'

His eyes danced. John Carruthers was himself again. 'Ever try to find a text with the word bridge in it, Freckle-face? It can't be done. It can't be found in either Old or New Testaments, though I believe that one of the books not included in the Bible as we know it had a reference to a natural bridge. I suppose it was something like our natural rock bridge in the Kawarau Gorge. I see Charles has got held up. You see, rivers served as tribal boundaries and military territorial lines. Does that sound strange? It oughtn't to, up here at Dragonshill where two rivers and the Great Divide itself are our natural boundaries. And the streams in the East were easily forded most of the year.

'And anyway, though it was decent of you to say so, my own tribute will be in the bridge itself. Tonight belongs to Madame, to the young Charlotte Beaudonais and her François. Henrietta, stay this way, won't you? Because there should be nothing but accord to mark an occasion like this.'

Johnny stepped to his place beside Madame in her big winged chair at the head of the room, her white head shining against the faded rose brocade, above her a picture of François, tall, slim, young, standing beside his horse, with the Alps in the background against a cobalt sky. The groups in the centre of the room stopped talking and moved to the walls.

Henrietta saw Charles's hand reach down to Penny's and, looking across at Hilary, knew she had hers in that of Francis. And a peace, because of what Johnny had just said to her, descended upon her. For a moment of magic, Johnny's hand, in spirit, was in hers, and neither the Atlantic nor the Pacific rolled between.

The day had been hot and Johnny was in long tussore-coloured trousers, with a tussore shirt and a plain blue tie, and above it, in a face tanned deeply brown, his eyes burned bluely. His fair hair was bleached almost white at the stubbly ends, and as she watched, Madame smiled up at him with utter confidence.

Johnny said, 'This reading is to express what Dragonshill means to us all, what Madame means to us all, and is a salute to François Beaudonais and to the men and women who lived here before he did and whose descendants are here today.

'It is also a thanksgiving from us all for the inestimable privilege of having known Madame, and from having benefited by the love and wisdom and graciousness of more than a hundred years of living. I may have created a bridge, but Charlotte and François Beaudonais created a way of life, sustained and strengthened in all but impossible living conditions, by their steadfast faith in God.

'I just ask that tomorrow as you walk to the approach of the new bridge, in your mind's eye you see this sheep-station, not as it is now, with its garden a riot of colour and with its belts of larch and pine and fir, but bare and windswept, exposed to the full fury of the storms, as it was once, and entirely unproductive. But men of vision and indomitable courage came here and have made it a land of plenty.

'But there was something even greater than their courage, and that was the fortitude of their women folk, facing the perils of the wilderness at their sides.'

Henrietta was glad Deirdre wasn't here to remind Johnny that one woman at least had lacked the courage—and the love—to follow her man.

Johnny continued: 'I want to pay Madame a tribute that is all hers. George Essex Evans said it far better than ever I could say it, said it of Australian pioneer women....

"... And there are hours men cannot soothe, and words
    men cannot say——
The nearest woman's face may be a hundred miles
    away.
... For them no trumpet sounds the call, no poet plies
    his arts——
They only hear the beating of their gallant, loving
    hearts.
But they have sung with silent lives the song all songs
    above——
The holiness of sacrifice, the dignity of love."

'And I would like to include in this two lines from a much older poet, John Donne, who was Dean of St. Paul's in 1621. I thought of this tonight when Henrietta and I were remarking how beautiful Madame looked against the background of her chair. John Donne said:

"No spring nor summer's beauty hath such grace
    As I have seen in one autumnal face."'

Johnny gave a slight bow in Madame's direction, and to their delight, the watchers saw a faint rose stain her cheeks.

He continued, 'I am reading certain selected verses, mainly from Isaiah thirty-five and forty, the ones I feel best fit Dragonshill and all who have lived and loved and laboured here...

'"... they shall possess it for ever, from generation to generation shall they dwell therein...

'"The wilderness and the solitary place shall be glad for them; and the desert shall rejoice, and blossom as the rose.

'"It shall blossom abundantly, and rejoice even with joy and singing; the glory of Lebanon shall be given unto it, the excellency of Carmel and Sharon, they shall see the glory of the Lord, and the excellency of our God....

'"... for in the wilderness shall waters break out, and the streams in the desert.

'"And the parched ground shall become a pool, and the thirsty land springs of water; in the habitation of dragons, where each lay, shall be grass with reeds and rushes.

'"And an highway shall be there, and a way, and it shall be called The way of holiness....

'"... No lion shall be there, nor any ravenous beast shall go up thereon, it shall not be found there; but the redeemed shall walk there....

'" Comfort ye, comfort ye, my people, saith your God ... prepare ye the way of the Lord, make straight in the desert a highway for our God.

'"Every valley shall be exalted and every mountain and hill shall be made low; and the crooked shall be made straight, and the rough places plain....

'"He shall feed his flock like a shepherd; he shall gather the lambs with his arm, and shall carry them in his bosom, and shall gently lead those that are with young.

'"Who hath measured the waters in the hollow of his hand, and meted out heaven with the span, and comprehended the dust of the earth in a measure, and weighed the mountains in scales and the hills in a balance....

'"... They that wait upon the Lord shall renew their strength; they shall mount up with wings as eagles;

they shall run and not be weary; and they shall walk, and not faint.' "

As Madame led everyone in the room to utter the Amen, Johnny looked across at Henrietta. Their eyes caught and held across the crowded room.

Henrietta knew an upsurge of some emotion she could scarcely define. This was Johnny at his best, a Johnny she doubted Deirdre had ever known, fine and true. This was what bridge-building meant to John Carruthers. Engineers also weighed the mountains, balanced the hills, throwing steel and concrete across the chasms and making the crooked ways straight.

She had been wrong, utterly and foolishly and cruelly wrong.

His was too fine a life to be undermined by a woman who would not follow him into wildernesses when he had loved her and yet who even now would not let him be entirely free of her.

This was what Johnny had meant. Living alone as he did, he was afraid of his own self, afraid of the revival of his passion for Deirdre. He needed a wife, a woman he would love, even if never in the way he had loved Deirdre. He knew Henrietta had what it would take for his sort of life, that she would follow him. And even if Johnny Carruthers could not give her more than second best, she'd take that and deem it better than the half loaf. More than that, she'd count it worthwhile ... and to the discard with all her old foolish pride. As soon as these celebrations were over and they could talk it out, this would come to be.

Penny had decreed earlier that they must see it was not too late a night, for Madame. But it *was* late, after all, because Madame had made them all laugh by saying, 'I know it sounds very foolish, but then one is allowed to have a second childhood, *hein*? But me, I never have believed in putting a child to bed early on Christmas Eve ... they never sleep, now do they? Much, much better to let them tire themselves out.

Please, I do not wish to go to bed till I am quite ready for sleep.'

So they sat on, relaxed and happy, with Madame recounting for them the milestones of the years.

Finally Mr. Deaverhill yawned openly and said, 'Well, as I'm only sixty-nine, I think I must turn in,' and they all rose. There was quite a procession going up the long main hall, and Henrietta and Johnny were the last. Suddenly she saw Johnny reach out an arm towards the switch, and out went the light. She was seized, kissed hard and quickly, then released. The next moment he had silently switched it on, while the exclamations were still going on.

Henrietta heard Charles say, 'Heavens, this is as bad as the erratic behaviour of the power-plant. Just imagine if we had a cut now! I wonder what on earth could have happened.'

'We shall probably never know,' said Johnny solemnly. But as his eyes met Henrietta's they were dancing. Just as well Charles had turned his back again.

Henrietta couldn't help it. Her hand went out to Johnny's, took hold of his fingers, squeezed them. Their eyes met again, seemed reluctant to disengage. His lips smiled a little, and under that smile Henrietta saw for an instant, the lonely little tyke of years ago. She was conscious of a clamorous tide of feeling sweeping over her. Not cocky Johnny Carruthers any more, but Johnny who had no home, who needed her. Then she said a surprising thing, still holding his eyes, 'Will you hold this mood till the day after tomorrow, John?'

He whispered, 'I will, my darling Henrietta. Till the evening of that day, and it will be once for all. We've done with all this skirmishing. Remember that.'

She wanted to lie awake, to dream over it, to puzzle out the meaning of everything that had ever happened between them, to try in some way to relate this with

167

what she had heard from the barn ... but it had been such a long day, such a busy one, and she was drowsy and happy. Anyway, she'd given up struggling. Whatever Johnny wanted of her she would give, and perhaps find the half loaf better than no bread. If what he needed was protection against the revival of his old feeling for Deirdre, then she'd give it. Henrietta fell asleep smiling.

Madame's Day dawned in the perfect weather the forecasters had promised. Penny was up almost at the crack of dawn, starry-eyed and bubbling over with excitement. She and Henrietta made early cups of tea and sent them into the bedrooms, Charles and Johnny assisting. The four of them drank their own steaming mugs standing at the kitchen bench, watching the world outside.

Never had Dragonshill looked more lovely. The sunrise was loth to stop painting the clouds high above the peaks with mother-of pearl colours, soft rosy pinks and amethysts, and had gilded the old rock formation of the Dragon with light that winked back from its mica particles till it seemed as if it were indeed covered with scintillating scales.

The willows curved and drooped over the homestead brook to look at their own reflections, and below the house Lake Tekapo floated in its milky turquoise, reflecting snow-capped peaks under an azure sky. There it stretched, all the glorious, now richly producing acreage of Dragonshill Station, tawny-gold tussock, mighty shingle fans, gorge and clefts and tumbled shapes all about them ... the Witches' Cauldron, Thunderclap Peak, Mount Erebus, the Two Thumbs range, and Hurricane Point over which Penny, eight years ago, had dragged an injured and unconscious Charles, lashed to a sledge, to the safety of Dragonshill and Grand'mère, on her hands and knees in the snow some of the way.

With one accord they turned to look at the River.

The Pawerawera, the River of Dread ... to be dreaded no longer, because by the time the next winter was upon them, a shining arc would span its treacherous waters.

'That,' said Penny, waving a hand, 'is the most wonderful sight of all ... that mass of concrete slowly shaping, the steel reinforcing, the conglomeration of machinery....'

The ceremony was at ten o'clock and as soon as breakfast was cleared away, people began arriving. The river was very low, subdued and tamed. Great trucks and lorries drove through the river-bed, loaded with people; hampers were stacked on the long tables the bridge workmen had set up on trestles, huge white sheets were whipped on to the tables, and the women of the Mackenzie went to work putting out china and cutlery. The food would be unloaded later.

Madame appeared, fresh from Hilary's skilful hands, in a new gown of mulberry silk, glinting with Lurex, to be installed in the front seat of the Land Rover. Charles had suggested bringing across one of the cars from the garages across river, but Madame had demurred. 'The Land Rover is more fitting for this scene, Carl. But I must walk the last couple of hundred yards. That too is more fitting.'

The people of the Mackenzie Country lined each side of the newly constructed road. At first, as Madame got out of the Rover and began to walk up the incline there was a throat-constricted silence, then as their love for Madame and all she represented surged to the top, cheer after cheer resounded.

To them she represented the last living link with their own forebears, the only one who could actually remember the earlier, crude and cruel days ... at one end were the bridge-workers, and mirrored on each rugged face was a gentler look, as if they too were caught up in the romance of it all.

Madame was escorted by Johnny, her two grandsons, and the Cabinet Ministers. Just as she neared the bridge-head, much more advanced than they had ever hoped for, because the men had worked with such a will, small Charlotte Beaudonais-Smith tugged her hand from her mother's and ran to her great-grand-mama, pushing her father aside, and clutching Grand'mère's hand.

Madame looked down, smiled, said, 'That was all I needed, *chérie*, to give me the necessary courage to fulfil all my duties this day,' and relinquished Francis's arm also and walked on erectly with the child.

They stood there together, the two Charlottes, one with a century of living behind her, the other with scarce two years.

The politicians, out of deference to Grand'mère's years, kept their speeches short, then Johnny motioned to Madame. Still with Charlotte's hand in hers, she stood there and, obviously moved, yet in control of her voice, spoke to her dear neighbours of the Mackenzie for what could so easily be the last time. Then she pulled the cord that unveiled the plaque and gazed without tears upon it.

To keep in imperishable memory
the steadfast courage
Of François and Charlotte Beaudonais
who tamed the high country
And rescued it from barrenness into rich
and full production.

Just as the cheering died away a roar came across the sky.

Charles said with huge enjoyment, 'Look up, Grand'mère, this is your tribute from the topdressers. This was their idea. A royal salute, they said, to a great lady.'

Everyone put their hands up to shield their eyes from the sun and up they swept from across the river ... the three top-dressing planes that had done so much to bring these golden acres into greater production ... they made a perfect sweep across the newly formed road, well clear of the crowd, then opened the hoppers and out streamed not fertilizers, but rose-petals. . . .

Henrietta heard Johnny say to Madame, 'And the desert shall blossom as the rose' and felt tears of which she was not ashamed slipping down her cheeks.

There was nothing to mar the day. The little breezes that blew across the river-flats and against the Alps were only zephyrs, carrying no storm-warnings upon their wings, only the lovely scents of Penny's summer garden. The air was full of the sounds of happiness . . . children laughing, women chatting, men talking sheep and planes, the clink of ice in long tall glasses, the feasting and the merriment.

By five they were all gone, even the official party, ferried across the river that before another summer came would be bridged.

The rest of them were immensely tired, but Madame sat quietly in her big winged chair, dreaming, a little reminiscent smile playing about her lips.

Johnny ran the last of the helpers through the river, mainly the folk from the three homesteads between here and Tekapo. The very last to go were the Kings and Deirdre, Deirdre who had entered admirably into the whole proceedings and had not in any way attempted to steal the limelight. Not that—after what she had overheard—Henrietta would ever quite trust her, but perhaps after tomorrow night she would not be in a position to do Johnny any more harm ever again.

It was still twilight. It wasn't as late as they had imagined it would be, when the homestead became theirs again. Perhaps when Johnny came back he would ask Henrietta to view the stars . . . she was pretty sure of it. Both he and she had imagined some folk might stay on when they had set tomorrow night as their assignment for their own affairs.

The phone rang. Penny answered it, 'Henrietta, it's from Johnny. From the bank. The Kings' car has packed up—the starter motor is burnt out. He wants to speak to you.'

Johnny came straight to the point. 'We didn't know till the Llewellyns and all the rest had gone on ahead, so I'll take the Kings down to Pukewhetu. But listen.' He dropped his voice—so the others mustn't be far away. 'I'll be back in just over an hour. You and I have an appointment. Now that no one has stayed on at the homestead, the night is ours, and ours alone. Savvy? Be ready to slip out when I get back. Tell Penny we won't be in, not to wait supper for us. She won't be surprised, I'll warrant. Oh, here they are. See you later, Freckle-face.'

Henrietta had worn the blue suit with the fringe that she had worn to St. John's that morning in Wellington. She renewed her make-up, but very delicately, fingered Johnny's pearls, caressingly smooth about her throat, decided she would say nothing to Penny till the lights of the truck came across the darkening waters of the Pawerawera. Just as well, because there was another ring—for Henrietta again. Penny looked puzzled but sounded indulgent. 'It's that man again, Johnny Carruthers. Whatever can he want now?'

Johnny sounded savage. 'Talk about luck!' he fumed. 'You just wouldn't read about it. Something's bust inside *our* engine now! It's got me beat—bits of metal sprayed all over the show. One has pierced the oil sump. I'll have to stay here with the damned thing and get the breakdown truck from Tekapo first thing tomorrow morning. Wouldn't it! Look, I'd borrow Uncle Mike's truck and ride one of Llewellyns' horses through, but it's my bounden duty, of course, to get this thing mobile again as soon as possible. We've had a wonderful spell of weather, with no danger of the river rising, but even though it's so low, one can never tell, and this is the one vehicle we can't do without. Henrietta——'

She interrupted him with laughter. 'Johnny, Johnny, don't be so impatient! It will keep.'

He said, in a much lower voice, 'Yes, but will you? Look, Henrietta, can you put that mood of yours into cold storage and keep it there till tomorrow night? It will be a long job, that I do know. Probably have to get parts up from Fairlie, if not Timaru. But I should make it by nightfall.'

She said anxiously, 'Don't let them hurry it, Johnny. Lives depend upon that truck, and if it isn't done till nearly night, don't risk crossing in the dark. What did you say?'

'I said I've done it a dozen times in the dark.'

'Well, please, Johnny? Not this time. I can't bear you to risk it.'

He laughed, sounding well pleased. 'All right, I'll take no risks. Not now my goal is actually in sight. I—oh, darn it, there's no privacy here. Well, keep it on ice, like I said, Goodnight, Freckle-face.'

'Goodnight, Johnny.'

She fell asleep the moment her head touched the pillow. For the rest of them tomorrow would seem a day of anti-climax after the build-up of the past few weeks. But not for Henrietta. She had come to an understanding of herself and would take Johnny on any terms.

She woke in the dark hour before the dawn to find her room illuminated by the most lurid light, evilly emerald, violet, sulphur. She crossed to the window and pulled her curtains back, but she was too much a child of the mountains not to know from the appalling clangour outside what was happening ... a violent electrical storm was playing over the Alps and reaching its most terrifying fury in the Witches' Cauldron. A magnificent spectacle, one she and Godfrey and Johnny had often watched spellbound in the early years before their world had fallen to bits. But this time she could take no joy in the unworldly fireworks because in two short hours, after a rainfall like this, the River of Dread would be running bank to bank.

CHAPTER NINE

It was three days before the river went down. Henrietta knew it could have been much longer had it been a snow-thaw instead of a freak storm, but every hour seemed an eternity and she was cold with dread, anyway, about the condition the river-bed would be in after the flood subsided.

And Deirdre was still at Pukewhetu. Now stop it, Henrietta. Things are different now. You have an understanding with Johnny that only needs ratifying. This is the time for trust.

Johnny rang to report to Charles that in any case the repairs were going to take the best part of two days as the parts had had to be sent from Timaru and the road was cut in two places.

And all anyone at Dragonshill could say was that it couldn't have happened *at a better time*! Henrietta felt like screaming every time someone said it. Yes, certainly it would have been disastrous had it happened the day before the unveiling, but for one person at least, it was a cruel delay.

On the fourth day the river-grader came up, re-forming the track, tracing the scourings-out. Henrietta felt sick whenever she looked at the river-bed with twice as many streams as before, swirling still in places and with the quality of the unknown about the shingle bottoms.

She asked Charles so many questions about the condition of the river that he finally stared at her in sheer amazement. 'Harry, what's the matter? I've never thought you worried unduly about the river or you'd never have volunteered to governess up here. And darn it, when you consented, you didn't even know we were going to have a bridge within the year!'

Henrietta flushed scarlet. 'Oh, I just suddenly felt nervous, I suppose. I don't think I ever crossed it straight after a flood. I was thinking the quicksands might have shifted. And the truck has just been repaired. I hope they've done a good job on it.'

Charles, a line between his brows, said, 'Why, girl, those chaps at the garage know our lives depend upon that truck. They never let the apprentices work on it. They'd never let it out unless it was in first-class condition.'

Madame spoke from the doorway. 'But naturally she is anxious, the *petite*, and why would she not be?—With Johnny one side of the river and herself the other!'

Charles chuckled and went away 'Yes, yes, Penny's just the same. It's a great compliment to us.'

Henrietta's subsiding blush came up again. She said, 'Madame, I—Johnny and I—we——'

Madame interrupted without excusing herself. '*Chérie*, I *know*. You neither of you, you foolish children, have put it into words yet, have you? You neither of you have been entirely frank with each other. But only words can clear up what lies between you. I think you have both made bogeys of Deirdre and Godfrey. And bogeys belong only to the dark and shadowy places. They cannot stand the light of day. But I saw Johnny and you look at each other after he read the Scripture the other night and I knew all would yet be well with you.

'It took me back forty years. It made me feel as if François was very near, more than anything that has happened this whole wonderful week. It was always like that with us. We would exchange a look across a room, and suddenly we were in a world of two. I think you and Johnny have quarrelled sometimes, *hein*? I am right? Of course I am. I do not believe in the supposedly ideal state of never having had a quarrel. No, I do not. People are just vegetables, if it is true, as they say. But I do not believe it. François and I sometimes quarrelled, not too often, you understand, but it never lasted. We had only to catch each other's eye to laugh and to remember that we two were truly one.

'I know you are anxious about him coming back over the river after flood. Me, I know all about that. There was no river-grader in our day. But, *mignonne*, do you remember reading *Daddy-Long-Legs*? You do? Then you will remember that when Judy fell in love with Jervis she said—because she was terrified of all the terrible things that could happen to him—that she'd lost her peace of mind for ever? Then do you also remember that she added, "But I never did care much for just plain peace." Odd how that little sentence stuck in my mind. I have not always been courageous, Henrietta, even if they did extol me three days ago. There were many times when I railed against the sheer hardness of life here among the mountains. Then I would remember that if I had lived an easy life, with my parents in the beautiful, gentle South of England, I would not have had François. And when I read that, I realized I would never have enjoyed an uneventful existence. At least I lived.'

Henrietta leaned forward and kissed Madame. 'You're right, Madame. I will not wear myself out with useless fretting. And I will try to be brave and discuss very frankly with Johnny that which has kept us apart.'

The old eyes looked kind, and wise. 'And you may find that under all his bravado, Johnny Carruthers has a great want, a great longing to be loved. It would not hurt you to sink your pride, *mignonne*, and tell him that long ago you borrowed a poem out of an old woman's scrapbook ... to copy it out, I presume. Am I right? I think the time has come for Johnny to sing your summer in. And every summer to come.'

She laughed at Henrietta's startled expression, patted her cheek and moved away.

The next day, despite her many trips to the ford, she was away from the homestead when Johnny made the crossing.

Hilary had rung. 'Henrietta, the men are away up to the Aranui Ford with the glasses to see how the stock up there seem to be faring and the children went with them. So I'm on my own. I've done a stupid thing—walked into the door with a carving knife in my hand. It's not too bad, but I simply can't manage to bandage it firmly. I wondered if you'd come over. And if you could do the vegetables for dinner and make the pudding, I could manage the rest and the girls can dish out and wash up when they get in.'

Henrietta had run up to the lookout and scanned the far bank with the glasses. There'd been no sign of any dust on the river road, but she hated to go, though Hilary would never know it. She didn't feel like riding over, because stretch trews and a skivvy didn't make you feel very glamorous—when Johnny came home she wanted to look reasonably feminine.

So she called out to Penny that she'd take the small old truck over.

It took time. It was worse than Hilary had made out. She made her some tea, washed up the tea-cups and the dishes she used for making the pudding, put the vegetables in their pans ready for Hilary to switch them on, and departed from Two Thumbs.

As she ran the truck into the yard, she saw it: the four-wheel drive vehicle, standing by the brown barn. So Johnny was home, and instead of meeting him down at the ford she would have to greet him under the eyes of Penny and Madame.

But they were not in either of the kitchens or the dining-room. The door into Madame's sitting-room was closed. She heard voices and decided she would rather go to her room and perhaps Johnny would come to her. She couldn't wait for starlight. It would be agony to go on calmly assisting with the cooking of the dinner; then there'd be the dish-washing, helping with the bathing of the children, serving coffee. No, too long to wait. Henrietta didn't care if it was the storeroom again. And perhaps they'd not have need of many words. Explanations might not really help things. There had been too much said already. They ought to simply go into each other's arms.

As she hesitated she heard Johnny snort, his voice rise, 'Of *course* I love her. I *always* have. I've always loved her and always will. But till now she's been out of reach.'

Madame's old voice was too faint and far away for her to hear the answer. Henrietta strained every nerve to pick it up. Penny sounded as if she were expostulating (as well she might be), but not a word was clear. Johnny started to say something else, but got cut short by the telephone bell.

Henrietta was standing transfixed by the dining-room table, one hand leaning heavily on it. She heard Penny say, 'It's for you, Johnny——Pukewhetu.'

Then Johnny's voice, in an impatient tone, 'Yes ... John here.' Then a sharp, incredible note, 'Oh, no, Queenie, no! She can't do that to me. Not right now. She can't. Queenie ... an hour or two can't make much difference. Doug can take her to Timaru later on. Queenie, you just mustn't let her go. It's devilishly important to me. No, don't discuss that with her. Just tell her she's *got* to wait till I get there.'

Henrietta came to life, flew across the room and managed to get into the hall. Johnny would go through the kitchens. She couldn't face him ... or anyone.

Three days at Pukewhetu with Deirdre and all the commonsense plans he was making for a future life with a commonsense wife had gone by the board. He'd almost, but not quite, deluded himself into thinking he was master of his emotions. It sounded as if Deirdre was going back to Christchurch. Perhaps Rodney was coming home and Johnny couldn't bear her to go back to him. This then was finish. For Henrietta.

Meanwhile she felt like a hunted creature. She must go to earth. No one must see her till she had gained control of herself.

She let herself out of the seldom-used front door and gained the shelter of the Douglas firs at the far corner of the garden. From them she saw the truck on its way to the ford, driven hard. She knew no fears this time about him crossing the river. She felt nothing at all, neither for him, nor for herself.

She felt bludgeoned. She only knew she could not go back into the house again. They would suppose she had stayed on to help Hilary. She would slip down the larch path and along the track that led to the head of the lake. Nobody was likely to come that way today. The men were up the Aranui valley.

How long she sat on an outcrop of rock above the mouth of the Aranui where it tumbled its waters into the turquoise immensity of Lake Tekapo, she knew not. All was turbulence when first it met the lake water, then gradually white water became blue, and froth subsided into a still, peaceful sheet of water.

Might she herself ever feel that way again?

When she was sufficiently under control she decided to stroll back to the house. No one must suspect she knew. They would tell her Johnny had had to go to Tekapo, probably. They wouldn't tell her the truth. And Madame would be sad for her, silently.

She was almost to the Rock of Ages when she saw the cloud of dust. She couldn't believe it. Not that he'd had time to go there and back. Oh, she had it ... when he'd got to Queenie's, he'd found Deirdre had not waited. So perhaps Deirdre was true to her marriage vows after all. Though that couldn't affect Henrietta now. Deirdre's feelings and loyalties didn't matter. Johnny's did.

She suddenly realized that although she could have faced Penny and Madame, she couldn't face Johnny yet. Oh, if only she were not at Dragonshill. She'd have to go through the agony of watching Johnny try to get out of their assignation for tonight ... if it had been anywhere else but Dragonshill with an as yet unbridged river, she could have taken the little old truck and gone away. But only the men were allowed to drive through the river.

She turned up the track to the Rock of Ages, conscious she was in view of the house windows for a few yards and hoping desperately no one would see her. She came up on to the grassy ledge at the back of the Rock and slipped into the balcony-shaped overhang through the cleft. It looked away from the house right down the lake. There were only mountains and a sky already showing a hint of westering gold and the small island, floating like a dark pendant on the breast of the lake, where once long ago, she and Johnny had been marooned.

Well, that was that. She'd wait here till she was quite mistress of herself, then go down to the house and pretend she was just back from Two Thumbs. Later she'd ask Johnny could she see him for a few moments. Would say she'd thought things over and it was just no go. She would be very prosaic, very convincing. It would let him out without a loss of face. He would be glad. There were limits to what a woman's pride would take.

Henrietta, some time later, took one last strengthening look of mountains and lake, then, filled with a deadly calm, turned to descend the rise. She went through the cleft to join the track, then stood there, half hidden by the pillar of rock, immobilized by what she saw ... *Johnny bringing Deirdre here.*

Of all the humiliations Henrietta had ever endured, this was quite the worst. There was just no way of escape short of hurling oneself over the balcony rocks on the other side. She felt as if her mind seized up.

Deirdre didn't have the right sort of shoes on for a climb like this. She wouldn't have! So Johnny was solicitous to the point of being faintly ridiculous. His arm was under Deirdre's and he was guiding her round every rock as if she were made of eggshell. Oh, Johnny,

Johnny, what a fool you are! What it meant she couldn't think, didn't even want to try to fathom it. None of it made sense.

She was caught in a trap. The Rock of Ages ... what was the line? '... cleft for me, let me hide myself in Thee'. But there was no hiding. What on earth did Johnny want to bring Deirdre here for? He must have no finer feelings. He—Henrietta stopped castigating him and began to move. She wanted to postpone the inevitable moment of discovery as long as possible, so she retreated, going through the cleft to the balcony, with the great height of the pillar rearing up behind her. She backed against the rock wall, a hand each side of her, as if she must try to get as far as possible from them. She knew by their icy feel that her cheeks must be blanched, that her eyes would be staring darkly out of a white face. There was just nothing she could do but face them.

Then, unbelievingly, she heard Johnny's voice calling *her* name.

'Henrietta ... Henrietta ... we know you're up there. We're coming up, Deirdre and I.'

Her eyes widened. What——

Deirdre came through the cleft first and said nothing. Johnny was positively pushing her. Then he was through and there was the oddest look on his face, a sort of ... sort of triumph, mingled with desperation. A no-nonsense, here's-a-confrontation sort of look. Henrietta was too numbed, too embarrassed to sort it out.

She took refuge in talk that didn't matter. 'How did you know I was here? I—I just——'

Johnny made an impatient gesture. 'It doesn't matter. Though it was Madame. She saw you.'

He swung round on Deirdre. In that confined space they were all too close together. 'Go on,' he said, 'tell her. Tell her that every word I told her about you and me was true.'

Henrietta leaned back against the rock because her

legs were only just supporting her, still with a hand each side as if she would draw strength from contact with its ruggedness. What had Johnny ever told her about him and Deirdre?

Nothing. Exactly nothing. Then what——

Deirdre didn't look as if she were being coerced. She looked as if she wanted to tell. She put out two hands to Henrietta who, if possible, shrank even closer to the rock. So Deirdre dropped them with a helpless gesture and said, 'Henrietta, you *must* believe him. You *must*. It was all true, every word he told you. You can't go on letting this affect your lives to the very end. You can't. I'd no idea or I'd have backed him up long ago.'

Henrietta stared, swallowed, blinked. Then she managed to say faintly, 'I'm afraid I haven't the least idea what you're talking about.'

Then it was their turn to stare.

Then Johnny said furiously, 'Don't be so ridiculous. You've *got* to face up to things, got to accept my word. After all, you had it in black and white. In my letter.'

Henrietta straightened up. She had been sagging. She stood rather erect. There was a little more life in her tone, though it was bitter rather than angry.

'Yes, I had your letter—about the most prosaic letter ever a girl had, proposing marriage, offering me your second-best. Not a word of love, *not one*. It was nothing less than an insult. Yet you expect me to—what's the matter? Why are you looking like that?'

Johnny pulled himself together by a visible effort, said, 'Look, let's get this straight. I'm talking about my *first* letter. Surely you didn't expect me to say it all over *again*? No one could have said it more clearly than I did in that first letter, the letter you never even answered. A letter fourteen pages long! Oh, I know I said that if you felt it was too soon to discuss it, not to worry, but you've never even——'

He got no further. Henrietta held up her hand, because just then speech was beyond her. When her stiff lips began to obey her mind at last, her eyes lost the dazed look and warmth began to flow back into her cold cheeks.

She said clearly, slowly, '*First* letter? What letter? I never had but one, asking me to marry you. Just a bald question. Offering me your second-best.'

Johnny looked as if he were carved out of rock too.

Deirdre flashed round on him. 'Don't stand there boggling, you great idiot! Get on with it. Don't you see? It's not that she didn't believe you—she doesn't know that *you* broke off the engagement, not *me*. She's *never* known it. The letter must have gone astray.' Then she gave a strange, wavering laugh. 'Oh, dear, it looks as if I'll have to do it. How awful! Henrietta ... he thought you wouldn't believe it unless you heard it from me. And now Johnny, of all people, has gone dumb. All right. Listen, Henrietta, listen, and don't move, or interrupt till you've heard me out and I'll go back to the house by myself. Johnny, I'll pick my way very carefully, I promise you. I won't do anything to risk a fall and hurt my baby. I've waited too long for it. But you and Henrietta must be alone.'

Baby ... then Deirdre ... something exploded in Henrietta's memory. Johnny saying Deirdre had longed for something for a long time. It was simple as that. A baby....

But Deirdre was sweeping on. 'Henrietta, that spring I came up here I was hurt and reckless and quite off-balance. Rodney had dropped me—the only man I'd ever really loved. I used Johnny—it was wicked and cruel and beastly of me, but I was so spoilt and selfish. I knew Johnny was in Christchurch and I hoped to make Rod jealous. It didn't work. Oh, Johnny fell for me in an infatuated sort of way and I got him to announce our engagement. That, I thought, would save my pride. I'd always had the boys falling for me from schooldays on, and I couldn't take it that the man I really wanted had seen through my shallowness. Oh, I know very well what I was like. Johnny, of course, had no idea, he hadn't even heard of Rodney. Then—this is what he told you in the letter that never reached you—he came to my parents' home one night and shut himself into the sitting-room with me and told me he couldn't go on. That he felt no end of a bounder, but he had realized that it was nothing but infatuation and that he loved *you*, the little pal of his schooldays. That he'd seen you crossing Cathedral Square the day before and had come to his senses and realized there was only one woman for him. You.

'All I could think of was my own humiliation, that being jilted would lower me still more in Rod's eyes. So I pleaded with Johnny to let it appear as if I had broken it. We could pretend I had realized I just couldn't take his sort of life. No one would be surprised at that. He was just going off to Malaya, a place thick, at that time, with terrorists. Everyone said they had known it wouldn't work.

'Johnny, of course, being chivalrous, didn't rush straight off to you. As far as he knew you'd never looked on him as anything else but a boy you'd grown up with, so he thought he'd give it a little time. He was to be away six weeks. But the job took longer than that, and before he could do a thing he heard you were going to marry Godfrey. He took off for Korea, and mail took a long time to catch up with him. Anyway, the next letter told him Godfrey was seriously ill, then that he had died. Only since I've been staying with Queenie have I heard the full story. I'm inclined to think you married Godfrey *because* he was ill. Queenie thinks so too. She says it was always Johnny with you. In fact, she handed Johnny a bit of proof tonight. It made his blood leap. Poor Johnny, what a mess we two made of his life between us—but it wasn't your fault. You never got the letter. Johnny will be able to tell you what was in it when I leave you, but not yet. Oh, no. I'm going to make quite, quite sure you've got it straight even if he's getting so impatient he'd like to hurl me over the edge.

'Six months after Godfrey died Johnny wrote to you

from Korea telling you the whole story. Said he had no idea how you felt about him, that he knew it was too soon, but that he just had to tell you he loved you and was prepared to wait till you'd got over Godfrey's death. That's just the bare bones of it ... Johnny will fill in the really wonderful bits for you when I've gone. Poor beggar, he was getting desperate. He even tried to make you jealous of me when I first came up here. I told him it was stupid, though I did try to play up to him at first hoping to rouse you.

'Seemingly, over the celebration time he thought you were softening. Then today when he got back over the river, he had a long conversation with Penny and Madame. Madame confessed she had asked me up here simply and solely because she thought if you saw Johnny and me together you'd know we hadn't an atom of feeling left—like that—for each other. You see, Madame has seen me with Rodney and knows there's no one else for me. But both she and Penny informed Johnny that they thought you still had doubts about Deirdre. That that was all that held you back. Johnny said how the hell could you—that he'd told you by letter long ago that it had been only infatuation and that he, not I, had broken the engagement. So he told them you had evidently not believed him and decided that he'd get me to tell you, but before he'd even had time to finish his discussion with Penny and Madame, Queenie rang to say I was going.' Deirdre grinned. 'You know what Johnny is ... a man of action. I'd had a cable to say Rodney was coming home a week earlier and of course I wanted to be at Harewood to meet him. I wasn't worrying about not saying goodbye to Johnny —I was absolutely furious when Queenie said he had ordered me to stay. I was all for going willy-nilly, but Doug wouldn't take me—thank goodness—he said if Johnny had done just that, he'd have a darned good reason. I said it had better be good ... and it was! I've said my piece, Henrietta. Do you believe it? Do you?'

Henrietta's eyes were shining. Every bit of her had

come to vibrant life. 'I believe you, Deirdre, oh, *how* I believe you. Deirdre——'

She was stopped again.

'I'm off. The rest is over to you two. Charles will take me back over the river. See you in Christchurch some time. I'll get the Llewellyns to take me to Pukewhetu. Oh, wait till I tell Rodney this, he'll be as glad as I am. Goodbye for now. I shall expect an invitation to the wedding.'

Henrietta said, 'Johnny, take her back through the cleft.'

Johnny did.

Then he came back.

Henrietta was standing just as he had left her, looking hungrily towards the opening. One stride and he caught her outstretched hands. He didn't fold her into his embrace instantly. He looked down on her, his bulk towering above her, his eyes searching hers.

Then he said quite brokenly, 'Oh, Henrietta, my darling, darling Henrietta, the things life can do! Oh, how I've wanted you ... and you me ... that's true, isn't it? You've wanted me?'

'*Wanted?*' she said, and her lip trembled. 'There isn't a word could say *how* I've wanted you.'

He smiled, unreservedly, 'Then suppose we dispense with words?'

She went into his arms, was caught, held against him, kissed as she had always longed to be kissed by Johnny, and, knowing no restraint now, responded to him, kissed him back.

He released her a little, looked down on her, said, 'Phew! That was worth waiting for! I knew you had that in you, but I couldn't unlock it. I could go mad, clean mad, thinking you never got that letter. Can't you imagine how infuriated I've felt? I thought you so unnecessarily cruel at times, and couldn't understand why. I thought that even if you couldn't love me in return, Godfrey's death ought to have softened you. I wondered why you couldn't be sorry for me, be more gentle with me when you turned me down. Henrietta, I can't remember the terms of that second letter—the one you got. How the hell did I put it that you could so misunderstand me? You said something about second-best. I remember that. I meant I knew I could never take Godfrey's place, that I wouldn't try to. Only I thought we could make a reasonably happy marriage. I planned to *make* you love me back.'

'I know that now, Johnny darling. I've still got the letter. I'll show it to you. Nothing matters now except that I know now you loved me all the time.' A thought struck her. 'You said Queenie offered you proof. How could she? I mean——'

He drew something out of his pocket, a smoothed-out piece of yellowed paper. 'When I rushed in, found Deirdre ready to leave, storming at Doug because he wouldn't take her, I didn't care that I had an audience. I just simply demanded that she come up here to tell you that I was the one who had broken the engagement and why. That seemingly you hadn't believed me, though I'd written and told you that. I went on to say I wouldn't try to take Godfrey's place with you, but I was sure you could love me in a different sort of way, if only I could persuade you I didn't just want a wife who could take my kind of unsettled life.

'Queenie made me sit down. I could have choked her at the time. I was in no mood for sitting. I'll never forget it. It was so gallant of her—Queenie's gift to both of us. She went away and came back and said in front of them all, 'Henrietta always loved you, Johnny. It was always you. But she thought Deirdre would always be in your heart. She thought you were a one-woman man just as she was a one-man woman.

'"I don't think she would ever have married my son had he not been ill and needed her so desperately. And it gave him great happiness. But one day, long after Godfrey died, Henrietta was here for a holiday. I knew she was breaking her heart for you. Other people put it down to grief."'

187

Johnny paused in his recital. 'Then Queenie said, "You know how Henrietta has always written poetry?" I nodded. Then she said, "When she'd gone away I found this in her wastepaper basket. If you read it you'll realize it couldn't have been written to Godfrey." Here it is, Henrietta, just as she gave it to me.'

He passed it over. Henrietta wondered just which poem it might be. She'd written so many to Johnny ... and burned them all. It was called: 'Extravaganza'.

She read:

> '*God must have loved blue best of all,*
>   *For blue He made the skies;*
> *For blue He made the thundering seas*
>   *And for a blest surprise,*
> *He kept the bluest blue of all*
>   *For your dear, laughing eyes!'*

She looked up into those dear blue eyes ... burningly blue they were tonight. Yes, Queenie would have known. Godfrey had had brown eyes. Dear, dear Queenie!

Johnny said, 'I liked the title. "Extravaganza". Love *is* extravagant, even ridiculous. Oh, when I think of all the foolish, extravagant things I've always wanted to say to you! It will take a lifetime. Oh, Henrietta, I know one doesn't cold-bloodedly take a carbon copy of love-letters, but how I wish I'd taken one of that. Imagine telling a girl you loved her ... I really let myself go ... and knowing that the darned letter is probably gathering dust in some dead-letter office, or was reduced to ashes in a mailbag fire! Oh, why didn't I insist on an answer either way? But never mind. Henrietta, will you ever forgive me for the way I turned on you that night when I first found out you and Godfrey had never been man and wife? Later, of course, when I'd cooled off, I was intensely glad that you'd never been a wife in anything but name, but all I could think of at that time was that you'd not cared enough, hadn't had the decency to tell me.'

Henrietta put up a hand to his cheek, said, 'Oh, there's no talk of forgiveness between you and me, Johnny.' She shut her eyes, said, in a tone of anguish, 'Oh, the things I've said to you! I thought you were still hankering over Deirdre ... I thought you'd just *got* to cut her out of your affections ... another man's wife. That's why I said she couldn't have loved you, or else she'd have followed you into the jungles and swamps '

Johnny's lips twitched in the old remembered way ... with no wryness, no bitterness. She reached up and kissed him. He kissed her back, then held her off from him and said, his eyes smiling bluely, 'Then you will follow me there? It will mean roughing it in a way you've never roughed it before. It may mean separations just when you need me most ... when our babies are being born ... you'll never have that stable, settled existence you and I both longed for as kids. You won't be able to put down roots.'

Henrietta reacted immediately, her eyes flashed, 'Johnny Carruthers, how dare you! Of course I'll follow you ... haven't you any idea how much I love you? Let me tell you——'

He had a hand over her mouth. 'Wheesht, firebrand! I just wanted to test you out.' Then a light came into his eyes. 'Because after all, there's no need to follow me. I'd made up my mind that I'd have you on any terms, Henrietta, that I'd not expect what you'd once felt for Godfrey, and I knew it was within my power now to give you exactly what you've always dreamed of. Oh, I know now that you'd follow me, taking it all in your stride, but—but there's no need.'

He leaned out over the ledge, drawing her with him and pointing.

'Henrietta, see the larch grove down there, under the lee of Fortress Hill?'

'Yes?' Her tone was mystified.

'Since all this topdressing and oversowing by plane came into the high country stations, Dragonshill, with many others, can carry more stock, both sheep and cattle. It's too much now for Francis and Charles. They're leasing me from there down to the lake, with rights and access to the summer basins. Can't you picture it, Henrietta? We'll build a home like those we loved in Switzerland ... a brown wooden house, with white sills and with boxes of geraniums that we'll take inside when the frosts begin. There's the perfect setting for it in that three-sided clearing in the larches. It will give us a garden naturally terraced ... and we'll grow all the alpine plants. And if you want roses, sweetheart, I'll build you a shelter fence. And from our bedroom window we'll see sunrise and sunset over the Lake. And the Dragon can brood in his kindly fashion over our house too. Remember what Penny always says? That he's a friendly family dragon like a Chinese dragon.'

She clutched him. 'But will it satisfy you? Won't you want to build bridges? I'll go wherever in the world you want to go.'

He laughed. 'No need, I'm being retained as a consulting engineer within New Zealand, and anyway, there are all the small linking bridges to be built here, among the mountains. I won't be satisfied till every family in this area has road access. Those ventures will give us the capital to stock our own place. Though we'll take a trip to Switzerland first ... that's what I nearly said that night we found out we'd both stayed in Brunnen ... that I'd take you back some day.

'But this is our kind of life, right for both of us. Where our children and our children's children will live, if they want to. And now, girl, we're going down to the homestead, to put those poor, bewildered folks' minds at rest. Poor Madame! She had even rung Queenie when I was tearing through the river to stop Deirdre going away, to tell her about you pinching that poem out of her scrapbook. Oh, Henrietta, I'll sing your summers in for the rest of your life.'

They were surprised to find the truck still in the yard and Charles there. He grinned as he noticed their linked hands. 'Well, thank heaven,' he said, 'that you've resolved your difficulties at last.' He said to Henrietta, 'I was terrified he'd take off again for the wilds of South America, and we could do with him on the estate. I take it, though, we'll have to advertise for a governess.'

Johnny shook his head. 'No. She can teach the kids till the bridge is finished. We'll be married right away, of course. When the bridge is open we'll fly off to Switzerland for a holiday. When the bridge is built you'll find it easier to get staff. But why hasn't Deirdre gone?'

'Because she wants to make quite sure it's signed and sealed. Go in and satisfy her, will you? And Penny is wringing her hands and wearing out our new carpet. I'll take Deirdre over when she's quite convinced.'

They went in to Madame's sitting-room, entirely unembarrassed. They went straight to her chair.

She rose, as erect as ever, and held out her hands to them both.

'I can see it is well with you, *mes enfants*,' she said. 'God bless you both, through all the years to come.'

Then her naughty black eyes twinkled. *Ma foi*, but how happy I am! It seems that even an interfering old woman still has her uses. Me, I am a matchmaker ... perhaps the oldest matchmaker in the whole world!'

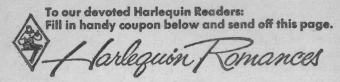
MAIL THIS COUPON TODAY